CREED

D1613273

CREED

MARGIAD EVANS

With an introduction by
Sue Asbee

WELSH WOMEN'S CLASSICS

First published in Great Britain by Basil Blackwell, Oxford in 1936
First published by Honno in 2018
'Ailsa Craig', Heol y Cawl, Dinas Powys, Wales, CF64 4AH

1 2 3 4 5 6 7 8 9 10

Introduction © Sue Asbee, 2018

ISBN: 978-1-909983-72-4 print
ISBN: 978-1-909983-73-1 ebook

Published with the financial support of the Welsh Books Council.
Cover painting: *Dowlais from the Cinder Tips, Caeharris* c. 1936
by Cedric Morris by permission of Cyfarthfa Castle Museum & Art
Gallery, Merthyr Tydfil and Mr Robert Davey, the Estate of Cedric
Morris.

Introduction

SUE ASBEE

Peggy Whistler (1909 – 1958) took 'Margiad Evans' as her pen name when she published her first novel *Country Dance* (1932). The name expresses her sense of being 'of the border', rather than Welsh or English; it sums up her love for the countryside around Ross-on-Wye where her family lived from 1921, and which had a profound effect on her sense of identity and her writing. Evans wrote novels and short stories, as well as poetry and essays. She was also an avid journal and letter-writer and those manuscripts that survive provide a rich insight, alongside her published work, into her deep and mystical relationship with nature, the intensity and complexity of her feelings for the border-country, her family, her lovers, and the often turbulent and conflicting emotions all of these evoked. Her autobiographical fiction *The Wooden Doctor* (1933) came after *Country Dance,* followed by *Turf or Stone* (1934*)* and *Creed* (1936). *Autobiography* (1943) is dedicated to her husband, Michael Williams; it describes in detail her relationship with nature, with many passages taken directly from her journals. *A Ray of Darkness* (1952), her last published work, is a remarkable account of the diagnosis and treatment of her epileptic seizures, the illness from which she eventually died in hospital on her forty-ninth birthday.

Creed, the last of Evans's novels, is probably the most challenging and ultimately the most thought-provoking of the four. It does not offer an 'easy read', nor did Evans intend it to. *Creed* takes suffering as its subject matter, and powerfully and dramatically it questions and debates notions of belief, fate, religion – and sin. The novel opens with a self-lacerating sermon by Ifor Morriss, a self-confessed drunken, disreputable, dishonest Welsh parson who, basing his sermon on a verse from the Book of Job, proclaims to the congregation his belief in the fundamental holiness of each individual, no matter what their wickedness. The effect on the congregation is profound (there are only nine of them): they are 'aghast'. But one man in particular, Francis Dollbright, is outraged. He follows the parson home and denounces him as a blasphemer. Up to this point Dollbright has been, quite simply, an unthinking regular churchgoer, but the effect of this particular sermon on his imagination is extraordinary and profound. The more he dwells on it, the more intolerant and moralistic he becomes. As a matter of principle he resigns from his job because John Bridges, his employer, lives with another man's wife. Dollbright's wife, not unreasonably, complains that she can't see 'any connection between Mr Morriss's sermon and working for John Bridges' and readers might well feel much the same: Dollbright has been well treated for fifteen years in Bridges' employment. But he remains intractable even though his resignation plunges himself and his wife into poverty. Questioning the parson's religious views turns Dollbright's idea of the order of things upside down, the ground shifts beneath his feet, and the feet of those around him.

Undoubtedly *Creed* is intended to disturb and challenge its readers. Few of the novel's characters are attractive, while the neighbourhoods which they inhabit, Chepsford and Mill End, are not, to put it mildly, pleasant locations. There is a church steeple, but it has no real significance or presence in the landscape, it is simply echoed by the mill chimney:

> Down those steps a maddened lorry driver flung his wife, breaking both her legs; from this door a brawl started which finished half a mile away with one man hammering another's skull upon the pavement; over this squalid pub, reeking, ill-lit, two brothers fought, and one died, for its possession.
>
> Ha, what a town! What a vital, wicked, boisterous town, which beneath its vigorous life, conceals a black current of despair and misery, and what people! Wild, vehement, laughing, whose two hands are generosity and vice, and whose eyes are weapons! (p.17).

Chepsford is Evans's depiction of iniquity, and in this novel her love of nature predominantly takes the form of weather: relentless rain and wind.

Seventy years after *Creed* was published and fifty years after Evans died her loving, affectionate sister Nancy remembered the novel with disdain, pulled a face and said that she had never wanted to read a book about a second-hand clothes seller. Nancy was thinking of the character Mrs Trouncer, 'very much like a mottled toad without the beautiful eyes. Her breath was dank as if her lungs were marsh plants' (p.27). Nancy failed to notice or else didn't appreciate her sister's extraordinary use of imagery and deft use of plain language. For example, although the description of Dollbright's country walk is a gothic and romantic expression of the extremity of his state of mind which lies firmly within a tradition of nature writing, Evans's acute observations lift the passage beyond common-place prose. Dollbright walks beside the river, which

> seemed to be pouring a ceaseless volume of water into a tunnel. The trees shivered as if no sun had ever touched them. The reeds and grasses were secret as a jungle. The wind was the only breath upon creation. The earth nursed it close, then it bounded from the lap and ran along the rim rapping a regiment of drums. Then it died, and the air drooped like a black flag from the heights (p.136).

Within a convention this may be, but the use of personification is unusual and imaginative. The movement of water, wind, earth and air presents a tangible sense of atmospheric conditions as well as implicit sound effects from the 'ceaseless volume' of water and the implied rustle of reeds and grasses. The military image develops the sound qualities, concluding with a drooping black flag, which lends the air oppressive weight. Evans's prose is rhythmic and poetic throughout; often the effects are deliberately far from beautiful, but they are as striking as they are fresh, and that is one of the novel's great strengths.

Perhaps Evans was responding to Nancy's criticism at the time of writing, when she wrote this self-defensive moment into her fiction:

> There are many I know who by this time will have picked up this book and put it down again. Having opened it, perhaps, read a page or two, they will pass their usual comment: 'Why write about such people?' I wish they

would read to the end. Maybe they would find a line of their own likeness, though no one is in my mind as I draw it. I own that *I* am here (pp.130-31).

That passage encapsulates one fractured realist convention, a moment of broken contract between writer and reader, for the third-person narrator has stepped out of the frame, owned that this *'I'* is the writer speaking directly to us, momentarily ignoring or forgetting the fiction. Readers are invited to see themselves in 'such people' as if this is a morality tale, yet in the next moment the speaker denies that her characters come from life. Boldly she then re-asserts her own presence in the work: 'I own that *I* am here'.

Evans is present in her text in a number of ways. On the face of it, *Creed* is a third-person narrative, but intrusive authorial interventions in the text, like the one quoted above, problematise the whole notion of author and narrator, raising questions as to whether this is a first- or third-person account, or if indeed that simply changes from time to time in the text. The novel begins in the third-person: 'Ifor Morriss was the Welsh parson of a large parish some three or four miles out of Chepsford'….It was winter, and turned out to be a wet night'. And the narrative continues in that vein. The narrator is omniscient, party to characters' private thoughts and conversations. That is, until the description of Mill End, at the bottom of Chepsford with narrow streets, 'the rattle of lorries…hissing of steam, and the churning of engines' (p.13) – a place of factories and production – when suddenly the narrative voice intrudes in the first person: 'This is Walls: when I live there I wonder whose eyes penetrate my windows' (p.14). That is a surprising and cryptic sentence, and much later we discover that a character in the novel, Benjamin Wandby, 'used to walk on stilts…proper ones, a yard high'. He looks into second-floor windows to discover folks' secrets with flour on his face, a top hat, and long trousers to cover the stilts (pp.41-42). This grotesque, nightmare figure stalks through Chepsford: 'People were very angry because they never heard me coming; even when I was watching them they didn't always see me. I was a lad on those stilts, I can tell you! I saw plenty of queer things' (p.41). Readers may or may not make connections between that odd first-person remark, with its suggestion of the conditional and the present tense – 'when I live there I wonder whose eyes penetrate my window'– and the stilt walker, mentioned in passing much later in the novel, who does exactly that.

This technique of occasionally (and surprisingly) dropping the narrator's omniscient voice and using 'I' is interesting. Evans was living in rural Herefordshire when she was working on *Creed*, apparently isolated from the debates of contemporary novelists and poets like Virginia Woolf and T. S. Eliot who were interested in exploring the limitations and the possibilities of language, of finding new ways of representing identity, memory, time, and the present moment in their writing. Nevertheless such preoccupations can also be traced in Evans's work. Such difficult but exciting concepts don't sparkle or advertise themselves on the surface of Evans's writing but they are all present in one way or another, providing evidence of deep thought about her craft. The short but cryptic preface to *Creed* demonstrates this. She asks how a writer can capture each moment, as nobody 'has ever seen any complete thing instantaneously….All we see is one thing moving upon another. And in trying to render them, we rely too much on juxtaposition for their fidelity'. She uses the image of a picture of a boat which *'floated'* – or appeared to – creating the illusion of overcoming the limitations of two-dimensional representation. That is what she tries to achieve in her writing:

> The reality of my manuscript is myself translating what I have learned into scribbled words on thin paper, pinned together with ordinary pins from a pink card, while the early day shines through the blind, as through an eggshell, and the dog in the stable raves at the chink of dawn under the door. (p.xviii)

By reminding us before we begin reading her story that it is an artefact, mere words on paper, she draws our attention to the process of writing fiction. She recreates the very moment she completes her preface by describing the light coming through the blind, the sound of the dog barking, and finishes it with the idea of constant change: 'What I offer you as reading is real, though I outstrip every page and at the end am different'.

There is another moment in *Creed* which may help to understand what Evans meant by 'real'. When the narrator interrupts a scene between Dollbright and his wife as they go to bed, the illusion that their relationship is real is deliberately destroyed, reminding us that this is fiction. It is only the *writing* of the story that can possibly be 'real'. This time, as the third-person narrative shifts into the first-person, Evans makes a comment that reflects on her own practice: 'This is an odd way to tell a story – a bad way. It splutters like a lamp with water in the oil' (p.56). This self-referential intrusion is another indication of Evans's interest in the craft of creating fiction; her evident appreciation of the limitations of language and the conventions available to her echoes those of her much better known contemporaries. The intervention 'This is an odd way of telling a story – a bad way' predates T. S. Eliot's lines from his poem 'East Coker' (1940): 'That was a way of putting it – not very satisfactory:/ A periphrastic study in a worn-out poetical fashion. Leaving one still with the intolerable wrestle/ With words and meanings'.

Reading Evans's journal entries contemporary with the writing of *Creed*, it is evident she had significant emotional difficulties to cope with over those long months. Her father was dying, indeed died, in the room above hers while for three weeks she was on her own in the house, taking care of him. It was not an easy death and it haunted her long after the event. He was an alcoholic, and in his illness he continued to drink: 'Whisky again,' she writes in her journal, 'He mumbles in his sleep: he holds horrible conversations with his loud dreams, I hear the rain, the crack of skylight, and his unearthly tones'; 'his mouth is the mouth of a dying man: it falls open like a grave. His arm lying outside the bedclothes and his poor curled fingers are scraggy as a dead fowl's foot'. Descriptions of the fictional alcoholic Mrs Trouncer in *Creed* – the whisky bottles hidden under her mattress and the horror of her delusions – may stem from Evans's own experiences of her father's addiction. But Peggy Whistler loved her father, while there is nothing loveable about Mrs Trouncer:

On her bed, in the dark, Mrs Trouncer was lying with crossed feet, in a ghastly stupor. Filled like a bloated sponge she was less asleep than steeped in reeking fumes. The sparks of consciousness exploded, madly amazed, fiery atoms too feeble to bring reason to the dizzy senses. Tomorrow she would lie there still, puffing out her lips and tugging at her ears, her yellow gaze fixed on her ultimate terror – death. (pp.29-30).

Menna, Mrs Trouncer's daughter, like Evans herself, is condemned to listen to the suffering: 'from her room she heard the moans and sea whispers, which continued all the night. It was a house of awful sights and shades which might stain the walls with the filmy silhouettes of appalling postures and deathly collapses' (p.30).

The journal entries from the period when Evans was writing *Creed* are tormented, often as emotionally charged as her fiction writing. She was in a passionate relationship with another woman, Ruth Farr; at the same time she was consumed by unrequited love for her publisher, Basil Blackwell, a man old enough to be her father, fond enough to give her the beautiful leather-bound journal in which she endlessly wrote to articulate, understand, and dramatise her life. It is no accident then that *Creed* is so emotionally highly charged. The characters Benjamin Wandby and Francis Dollbright are equally capable of lacerating themselves; for different reasons theirs too are tormented minds.

But *Creed's* violence and intensity has a literary forebear over and above any lived experience, and it comes from Evans's fascination with Emily Bronte. There is a curious dedication after the title page: 'To Flo from Lil'. This formalises the handwritten inscription inside the 1934 copy of *The Wooden Doctor* which Evans gave to her sister Nancy. They shared a number of nicknames and adopted different personas for their own amusement, so on the fly-leaf of *The Wooden Doctor* Evans refers to herself and Nancy by no less than four different names: first the book is from Florrie to Lil; then from Charlotte to Emily, and last, to Sian Evans from her sister Margiad. 'Emily' and 'Charlotte' refer to two of the Bronte sisters, and are followed by the inscription 'in honour of Nancy and Peggy's expedition to London 1934'. Interestingly Margiad casts herself as Charlotte and her sister as Emily, while it was actually Emily Bronte who haunted Margiad throughout her life. Illness prevented her from writing the book she planned about Emily, but her essay 'Byron and Emily Bronte' was published in *Life and Letters Today* (June 1948). There she argues that the two poets were 'affinities' with 'extraordinary similarity of diction…even to the constant use and close-set reiteration of certain terse and ordinary words – words which they invest with a vehement and vindictive purpose almost unique in letters'. Evans's argument is based mainly on Bronte's poems, not specifically her novel *Wuthering Heights*, which nevertheless she considers a masterpiece. But her interest in Byron and Bronte's use of language and ways in which they invest words with 'vehement and vindictive purpose' suggests her own register in *Creed*, which challenges *Wuthering Heights* in its relentless savagery.

Bellamy Williams and Menna Trouncer's destructive love affair of contradictions, rejections and jealousies may lack the motivating force within Evans's narrative that Catherine Earnshaw and Heathcliff's has within Bronte's, but it is still powerful. It rests less convincingly but just as destructively on Menna's promise to her mother 'to be with her anywhere' (p.126) even though, as Menna tells Bellamy, her whisky-sodden mother would 'rather put a light to me when I was asleep and burn me up than see me with you' (p.126). Mill End collectively considers their relationship to be a 'sort of fatal attraction mingled with tragedy' (p.117), and no wonder, as the image of Menna rouses Bellamy 'to hunger and furious rage', and they 'fought like tigers, with every cracking sinew' (p.119). When they finally spend the night together, unable to resist temptation and Mrs Trouncer's ultimatum, inauspiciously 'Bellamy's bedroom was cold as death, with a sweat of damp on the low ceiling' (p.163). The description of him sleeping while Menna watches is extraordinary. As the light of dawn illuminates his face,

> It seemed to rise from him, to break through the skin, like the loosened spirit lifting in the air. It might have been burning from some jet within the head which seemed to sleep in concrete, wrought and sealed in a statue. The hair fell back from the blank forehead and the neck lay like a fallen pillar (p.164).

This powerful portrait of life in death is achieved through the image of a broken concrete statue and the simplest of language: Bellamy's body is observed not as a whole, but in parts; these parts are not 'his', but become 'the skin', 'the head', 'the hair', and 'the neck'. Waking, he cries out 'in terror' because he has wasted precious time with Menna by sleeping. His remark after he tells her repeatedly that he loves her may fall short of the force and simplicity of Cathy's 'I am Heathcliff' in *Wuthering Heights*, but amounts to much the same thing: 'I *wish* you grew on me. I wish there were no flesh between us' (p.164). This unrealistic desire, together with the death of Menna's mother the following morning, ensures that though they may marry, their future holds no more promise than Catherine's and Heathcliff's. In *Creed* only the unmarried couple, John Bridges and Barbara Cater, lead a peaceful co-existence.

Florence Dollbright's breast cancer, crucial to the resolution of her husband's religious crisis, is cruel but it generates moments of kindness and sympathy in the savagery of the novel. Florence has female friends and neighbours. Long before Dollbright is told, Emily Jones feels the 'hard, seemingly movable substance' in Florence's flesh and sobs with her as she insists that it must have medical attention. Margaret Wandby sits with her, the landlady of the public house sends pasties and Emily brings pears, declaring 'you've got real courage, my dear' (p.89). Barbara Cater, who lives in sin and reads literary theory, sends a silk dressing jacket as a gift and a note wishing her a speedy recovery. When Florence puts the jacket on 'the wisps of her grey hair twined on the silk; her appearance was strangely clumsy and bedizened', but she straightens her neck proudly and says 'Well!' (p.89). Her fear of the operation to come and the description of her admittance to hospital are sensitively drawn, from her perspective as well as from her husband's. The kindness of the matron, the nurse, and the chatter of the other women in the ward eventually lift fear and responsibility from her as she lies in the cold bed, 'She had only to be still. Living and dying were not her works' (p.95). The delicacy of Evans's writing touch comes in moments such as Florence gazing at scarlet geraniums through the wires of a bird-cage; or from her longing for the bunch of violets denied to her, and her purchase of bottle of scent. Florence is shielded from the malignancy of her cancer, as was common practice at the time;

it is her husband who has to bear the truth, and it is he who has the last words of the novel as he defies and challenges God: 'From your millions you have lost me, and all your aeons will never bring me back' (p.178).

Evans lived her life on an emotional precipice, and turbulent feelings applied no less to her writing. Working on *Creed* she wrote in her journal: 'How I am tormented by not being able to get at my book, by words, similes, phrases of indefinable beauty which mock me like the skys and are blotted out by my fingers'. She was, perhaps, too close to the work to fully appreciate her own remarkable achievement in this passionate, unconventional and fascinating novel.

Further Reading

Evans, M., [1932] (2005) *Country Dance*, Cardigan: Parthian Books (Library of Wales)
Evans, M., [1933] (2005) *The Wooden Doctor*, Aberystwyth: Honno Press
Evans, M., [1934] (2010) *Turf or Stone*, Cardigan: Parthian Books (Library of Wales)

Bohata, K., and Gramich, K., (2013) *Rediscovering Margiad Evans: Marginality, Gender and Illness*, Cardiff: University of Wales Press
Caesar, K., (2012) *Margiad Evans: Body, Book and Identity: an analysis of the novels and autobiographical texts*, Milton Keynes: Open University
Dearnley, M., (1982) *Margiad Evans,* Cardiff: University of Wales Press
Lloyd-Morgan, C., (1998) *Margiad Evans,* Bridgend: Seren

I BEGIN to write, relying on the force and fine senses of each moment. That will be my strength. Nobody has ever seen any complete thing instantaneously. Such a vision would mean a pause, which there is not. All we see is one thing moving upon another. And in trying to render them, we rely too much on juxtaposition for their fidelity, and the reality of each separate point. That may be order; it is not creation.

A long time ago I went with an artist to look at an exhibition of pastels. I have forgotten all the pictures except one. It was not beautiful, not odd, not original. The subject was a boat lying silkily on a calm lake. But the boat *floated*: it was united with the water, not joined to it. That was reality. The reality of my manuscript is myself translating what I have learned into scribbled words on thin paper, pinned together with ordinary pins from a pink card, while the early day shines through the blind, as through an eggshell, and the dog in the stable raves at the chink of dawn under the door.

What I offer you as reading is real, though I outstrip each page and at the end am different.

MARGIAD EVANS.

CHIEF CHARACTERS

FRANCIS DOLLBRIGHT—An ironmonger's clerk
IFOR MORRISS—A parson
JOHN BRIDGES—Owner of the ironmongery
BENJAMIN WANDBY—A lodger at Dollbright's
BELLAMY WILLIAMS—A mill hand
FLORENCE DOLLBRIGHT—Francis' wife
MARGARET WANDBY—Benjamin's sister
GWEN TROUNCER—A wardrobe dealer
MENNA TROUNCER—Her daughter
and others

I

IFOR MORRISS was the Welsh parson of a large parish some three or four miles out of Chepsford. Here is a list of his public sins. He was dishonest; he was irreverent towards the formula of the Church; he got drunk; he knew disreputable people; he sent his money spinning the wrong way round.

He had good reason to reproach himself for his way of living. It came to his ears that certain of his parishioners were meditating a complaint to the bishop. Therefore he paid many visits during one week asking people to appear at church the following Sunday evening. This request was prompted by reasons as subtle as his own beleaguered character.

It was winter, and turned out to be a wet night. After all his efforts only nine of his parishioners and one man from Chepsford were in the church. When the time came to preach, Ifor Morriss went up into the pulpit, lighted the candles and looking down on the people, started a glib text, hesitated, stammered and was overcome by sincerity. The blood rushed into his head and his ears; he waved his hands as if to put back a force. But the spirit of Truth tormented him.

'I am going to pray.'

Kneeling he bent his forehead on his wrists. After a few minutes, he arose and announced in a firm tone:

'Job, the nineteenth chapter and the twenty-fifth verse: "for I know that my Redeemer liveth and that he shall stand at the latter day upon the earth." ' He stared frenziedly, not knowing, what he might say in this bare mood, but the surge

1

was too strong for him and he burst into unpremeditated speech.

'My father was a minister on the shores of Bala. He died at night in its violent waters because he would not shirk a call from the other side. Thus was his faith, his desire, his whole ambition—to be an exact tool of God. He was a stony, rigid believer, an inexorable teacher who inflicted religion on me like a punishment. I was forced to regard sinners as "lost"— I say *regard* and not *think*, for there was no thought in it. I had no more of religion than the sting of its tail; as a boy suffers the rod I suffered my father's faith, and bore only the stripes. I had no religion, I say; only fear, the fear of being cast out from the hope of reward and the meek bliss which my father promised to the obedient in the name ot his relentless inspirer. Only fear. Do you know what that means? Do you know what it is to have your judge come upon you like lightning, to blast you? Do you know what it is to be flat to the earth and be afraid to lift your face? To breathe in submission to an appalling hereafter, to see Hell beyond death and death at hand? To pray without hope and without comfort? To live on the margin of damnation in the torment of impotence; and to have your defencelessness hurled at you daily?

'I know. But with growth came the inevitable subterranean suspicions, the unuttered doubts, and at last a cowardly outward acceptance, which was a shell around a withered belief. Yes indeed, my faith rattled within me like a dried-up kernel which I ought to have spewed up and buried, but I was afraid. What enlightened me? You shall hear. There were one or two books in the Bible which I was ordered to study sparingly—this book of Job among them—because my father discerned in it a reasonable insurrection, and the lines of profound reflection. I did not read it with intelligence until I was nearly twenty, and then I shuddered in the dark at its power!

'At first that was all, but, gradually penetrating the fascination of its language I approached its devious and intricate meanings, until in time I was able to build my faith in the very desert where my father's had crumbled. And this was my foundation. Listen! *Job would not serve God in fear*. That's what I saw. That's what I have seen for nearly forty years.

'The book is almost throughout a record of transgression and pride, concluding in the utter harmony of submission and confession. It is a complex lesson, not easy to understand or interpret: it seems at times as though the writer is exalting Job's courageous obstinacy in his rebellion against the infallibility of the Almighty: as if a heart and soul were uplifted and sustained by the most daring and outrageous argument that could ever be imagined or uttered; an argument between manhood and divinity, between creation and the creator, between the one who is not aware of his days nor how they shall end, and the One Who spins the planets, gathers the frantic torrents into the sea and moulds the rim of the sun.'

Ifor Morriss bent himself and talked now as if into the breasts of his hearers.

'If, as Job, we possess the fearlessness which can plainly regard God as the supreme image of man, glorified indeed in virtue but himself in outline, then Job is a glass to ourselves. He speaks our bitterness, he seeks our rest, his despairing complaint is ours, his tragic dirge, his curse. His eyes, burning in the heat of cruel affliction, are our own. But we are not all bold. We do not struggle with the Lord that He should honour us as we honour Him; we do not require to be shown His command over the universe. Most of us crave for pity and pray for help.

'Yet one thing we may instantly recognize and claim as ours—all of us—and that is human pain and grief. There is a formula of grief visible to persons, but lacking the sharp inner edge. That is not what I mean. I mean personal suffering. Suffering cannot be without sensitiveness. Sensitiveness is a sign of fine creation within us, the print of God's hand, his Forefinger in our direction. *Bodily* pain is a sign that life remains and wrestles to retain its house: spiritual pain that the spirit is not dead. While it is able to writhe the spirit *cannot* be extinguished, the light of God *cannot* be quenched. That is an old truth which to my mind does not go far enough. Let us pursue it.

'Let us assert that the spirit which is hardened even to corporeal extinction is paralysed—that is diseased—and is still within the tender handling of our God. Listen to me, when I, a sinner and a fool in my ways, vehemently declare to you that repentance is good, but that without it still the soul may survive. We are immortal because God has touched us, because He has formed us for eternity and not for a span. Let us be clear eyed. Let us do away with false surface discrepancies born of antique scholarship and the *study* of holiness. The Old and New Testaments differ only in their teaching of law and ritual. The lessons they give us in spiritual living are marvellously unanimous. In support of the faith which I have just bared to you I could repeat whole passages from almost any part of the Scriptures. And these are rules expressed for human guidance, attainable by ordinary people! If man be capable of this selfless forbearance, is not God's a vaster certainty? If man forgive his own stumbling image cannot God Who adjures him to do it? Ah, I tell you man cannot perish! I know it, for God loves him; not as a saint but as a blackened sinner he is loved. I know it. I know that my Redeemer liveth. I know that my Redeemer is my soul.'

The candles shone into the hollow roof. Ifor Morriss threw out his arms and joined them across his breast as if he were both exulting and guarding a deep jewel within himself.

'I have come to my text,' said he. Which of you, taking leave of a beloved friend for ever, would not consider your last words sacred? They would dwell in your mind forever, fixed by the memory of your parting; they would be involuntarily true and tender. This verse of Job stands at the head of the burial service. It is the message chosen as our farewell to our dead whom we shall never see again as we saw them in life, reassuring, promising the final union in God. And it has been taken from the Old Testament to stand in the very centre of Christianity. But what did Job know of Jesus Christ? Nothing: he was not a prophet, he was only a smitten man having faith enough to see the end of his afflictions. He spoke those words not as a prophecy of Christ's coming, but as a declaration of what he knew the Lord had sheathed within his wretched foul carcase. His Redeemer was his own undying spirit in which was his creator, the Emperor of Eternity.

'Job was sure and honest in his bold faith. And it was this integrity that God honoured. Yet Job could sin. What a magnificent parable of ourselves if we can but accept it!

'Once when I was a young man with a hard heart I attended the assizes throughout the trial of a woman who had killed her husband. Hers was a monstrous and proven crime; she was sentenced to death, and justly, according to our penal code.

One would have expected to find brutality and depravity reflected in her features, or at least the fixedness of devilish resolution. And yet—there was the unconquerable divine mark transcending all else as the light of the sun! I could have wept, for guilty as she stood, condemned, the rope round her neck, the deed on her conscience, going to death in the frightful blackness of unconfessed murder, hard, perjured, cruel, she yet had the look of God. He Himself stood in the dock, and as surely as He was visible then He bore her through the miserable end of her body to Eternity....

'My friends, although we should be murderers and blasphemers, although we are eaten through with meanness, cowardice, deceit, cruelty and the unnamed sins of our lusts, we should never be afraid to lift our foreheads to His face: although we are conscious of a determined will to continue in our vile courses let us worship and say:

'"Lord, I know You are in me, and I thank You for Your presence." In the midst of our wickedness and our resolution to continue, let us kneel and avow: "I know that You have not abandoned me."

'I am not a man who has done well. You will say that my faith is easy to follow and I have taken full advantage of its breadth. If you have listened at all you may accuse me of being an unholy disciple of the Church. It comes to this:

'I believe that for us all there is no spiritual death or torment though we may have earned it. We are sinners, but our Redeemer liveth—He liveth *here*.' Ifor Morriss put his hand upon himself. Then in a powerful voice he cried along the aisle:

'"Have pity upon me, O ye my friends, for the hand of God hath touched me. And now to God the Father..."'

Abruptly turning towards the east he mumbled indistinctly and the aghast congregation watched him fall once more on his knees in the pulpit.

*

'Ifor!' exclaimed his wife, who was waiting for him outside the vestry door under an umbrella.

'Ifor, are you mad? What on earth did you mean?'

She ran up to him and shook his arm. 'Let me alone,' said he sulkily, breaking away from her. My throat's confoundedly dry, and I only spoke for ten minutes, too! I feel as though, I'd been immersed for an hour. My collar's tight … Come along. Don't let's squabble over my dubious sanity in this flood.'

As soon as they entered the vicarage he picked up the cat and carrying two bottles of beer, went and shut himself in his study.

He lighted the lamp, but it required filling and burned with a dry blue flame. Having undone his collar he started to think, meanwhile caressing the cat with his left hand. He was not long alone.

'A man wants to speak to you,' his wife informed him from outside the door.

'Oh, curse! Who is it?'

'I don't know, but I saw him in church. I think I'd better tell him to go away and you come to supper.'

'No, I don't want anything to eat yet. Bring him along, will you?' he retorted unpleasantly.

Mrs. Morriss went to the front door scornfully wearing her blue rubber apron. She held a candle which flickered along the naked stone passage. A man was standing in the porch. She showed him the study. He did not knock but entered immediately. Ifor Morriss was sitting at the table looking at the cover of a dusty book.

'What can I do for you?' he demanded truculently.

'Blasphemer!'

The visitor approached him, regarding him with a glare so hard and possessed by indignation that he lost his words. He recognized him as the man from Chepsford, who had been to his church several times during the last year. He was an elderly man, with grey hair, rather short but sturdy, wearing a stiff mackintosh, thick boots, and holding a righteous black hat. The point of his long nose cast a shadow over the whole of his mouth and chin. He continued to speak in a resolute voice, correctly but with a glow of strong anger:

'I make no apology, sir, for calling you by that name in your own house, though up till now it has been a custom of mine to lift my hat in passing one of your profession on the road. A demon must have tempted you to break out as you did just now in the house of God!' Ifor Morriss saw that he had trained his rigid gaze on a corner of the room. There was something peculiar in his eyes, as if he were crossing a narrow dangerous bridge and was guiding his feet by that straight final stare. The wind flaring in the cedar tree on the lawn seemed to add its own cry to his passionate presence.

'Who are *you*? What name may I call *you* by?' Ifor Morriss enquired ironically, rubbing his rough bluish cheeks with his fingers.

'My name is Francis Dollbright.'

'And what do you want with me?'

'You shall listen to me.'

'No orders!' said Ifor Morriss sharply, with an imperative sawing of his arms: 'Sit down and talk if you wish but keep civil or out you go. I'm willing to hear you—in fact, I've often wished my sheepish congregation *would* answer back. An argument's easier than a monologue. What do you want to say?'

'I want to show you what you've done, you, a chosen minister who handles the Sacrament.'

'Ah, you feel like a prophet, I suppose, come to rebuke me in the name of Jehovah,' concluded Ifor Morriss, filling another glass which he had produced from the mantelpiece where it held spills. He pushed it towards Dollbright, who shoved it back so roughly that the beer slopped over the rim.

'Sit down? Not I?' said Dollbright, unabatedly. 'Nor will I drink with you, nor loosen my coat, nor breathe near you.'

He struck his palms together, retreated from the table and fixed his eyes on another corner of the room.

'Are you afraid of seeing the devil behind my shoulder?' Ifor Morriss sneered.

'The devil is not behind you, but in you.'

'Don't you go thinking you're in the air looking down on me,' Ifor Morriss retorted. 'If I'm a bad parson you're a worse churchgoer to judge by your attendance. I've seen you in church five times, I think?'

'I'm a regular churchgoer. I visit as many churches as I can reach because I like to feel God in all His houses. But you have turned me against the Church that tolerates you and your kind.'

'Ah, I'm sorry for that; but your faith must have been wretchedly limp if I can take the starch out of it.'

'It's not you yourself, but that you're allowed under a holy roof. It would be just if your parishioners turned you out on the hills. I've been out there—there a man meets himself. You've filled me with doubts. How does the Church serve God? With ministers like you—*you*!'

'With unassailable faith,' Ifor Morriss avowed.

'With corruption and lies!'

'Be quiet!'

'I will speak! With blasphemy, abuse of the office and neglect of God's word. With selfish delusion and satanic insinuation—'

'Mr. Dollbright—moderation,' said Ifor Morriss, shaken by laughter, 'I am not capable of fulfilling your estimate. My failings have meaner names.'

'You're a branch that will crackle! You say the soul cannot perish, but I hold that evil may rot it quite away, or twist it to a monster fit only for the hell which, however, you may comfort yourself, is threatened by Christ himself to all backsliders. You *have* perished, although you can drink, sift money and blaspheme in the pulpit. You're a misshapen demon hiding in the cloak of a religion that you revile. Your spirit is dead.'

'No.'

'I say, yes.'

'No,' said Ifor Morriss assuredly.

'God in the dock!' exclaimed Dollbright with horror, his motionless eyes on a smudge on the wall, 'say rather God in the judge and jury who condemned that wicked woman. When she was hanged her eyes shut for ever on everything that was pleasant, and if her soul survived it was to undergo perpetual torment. We are told it: it is part of Christianity. And only Christ can save us—our only Redeemer. You have forgotten that God is not only our father, but our omnipotent judge. What's the use of being good if the wicked enter into the same reward?' he finished simply.

'First and second prize.'

'Answer—answer me!'

'I did not mention reward. I said the soul survived no matter what deeds it was responsible for during this life.'

'It does not, it does not survive. Or if it does, only in a vile shape.'

'The shape of a soul?' Ifor Morriss muttered thoughtfully, smiling at the idea: 'What is your idea of the hell where these deformities are tortured by the command of a disappointed Saviour?'

'Go to any menagerie: look at the lowest, ugliest beasts defiled by the earth and defiling the air and imagine in their hearts the picture of the highest and most ethereal existence that is possible and is denied to them.'

'I will go to Regent's Park,' said Ifor Morriss perversely, but he was beginning to appreciate the architecture of a sombre and peculiar belief.

'Why shouldn't it be like that? If a man lives badly he becomes coarse, bloated; his flesh decays, his bones rot. He is a distorted bulk, burns inside himself. He grows hideous and repulsive— dreadful to everybody. That end can overtake a man's soul. Then it goes to its own kind.'

'Do tell me, I am really interested—holding such views, what do you feel towards other people? Your neighbours, for instance. Do you like them? Some of them must seem lost to you. Doesn't their fate affect you?'

'They aren't in my hands.'

The parson looked up at Dollbright's darkened mouth.

'You speak through a shadow,' he said slowly.

'And the images of your damned thoughts blacken your forehead.'

Yes, it is smoked. I must trust to the penetrating eye of God. Well, go on, you miserable deadlock of a man, if you have anything more to say.'

'I have not.'

'I doubt if your creed is really as cruel as you make out. You would need to be more humanely heroic. I'd like to talk to you, but you'd no more listen to me than drink that beer. I pity you. You are sad. You came in here to pitch into me and you've been damnably rough in your wording. That's nothing: I've understood your motive and I respect it. *This* is what oppresses me and drives me frantic, this chaos, this intellectual analysis of what was once a raw and practical religion.'

He shook his thumb at a row of theological works in the bookcase.

'Look at it. There's despair. My head was clear once. No drink will bring a man to such a pass as reading. He is born with his own wisdom and it is driven out by such stuff as this. A man does not know what crosses his threshold. He opens his door and calls in a fiend. He doesn't know the woman he embraces; and least of all he knows the faith he declares. These are three things he will never know. But this I would swear: one moment of honesty and integrity is more enduring than a century of evil. Mr. Dollbright, you aren't aware of the power of good; you over-estimate the power of evil. I cannot understand why God has given us light and withdrawn it, honoured us with vision and limited it. The world is dark with the feebleness of our sight. We must be patient even in the face of death. Will you come and see me again?'

'No.'

Morosely Dollbright went towards the door.

'Then wait a minute. When you find that you can withhold your sympathy from urgent need, then you can be certain that God will abandon man to destruction. Good-night.'

Dollbright did not answer and a moment later he had left the house.

*

Ifor Morriss's idea of Dollbright's attitude towards his neighbours, though unvoiced, was fairly shrewd. But before going into this it is necessary to describe where and how he lived.

There is a part of Chepsford known as Mill End, at the bottom of the town on river level. It is a busy quarter more concerned with producing than buying and selling. The trading is done from hand to hand rather than across a counter. The mill chimney, with its blackened top and soot-smeared brickwork, throws an angular shadow across the roofs. The streets are narrow and gritty. Here the usual sounds are the rattle of lorries as they bump over the cobbles through the double gates into the mill yard, the hissing of steam, and the churning of the engines within the square red walls, a train clanking over the iron-plate bridge, and the persistent trickle of water under the lock gate.

All day long men gabble and guffaw, children squabble on the pavements, footsteps break in and out of hearing, the streets groan with the strain… . But at night … then the silence seems to broaden the spaces and lie hollow on the empty cross roads. The lamp which has thrown its fixed light upon the cracked plaster walls of the 'Bunch of Grapes,' goes out at eleven o'clock: in one second, with a click, here is the doom and act of darkness.

Early, early cocks begin to crow from the backyards; the low cocks calling the high cocks on the hills, measuring night distances. People are still about, one by one, solitary in their walking, who are strangers to the inhabitants, waiting for the dawn on their feet. The sleepers lie, the passers go by unaware. This is Walls: when I live there I wonder whose eyes penetrate my windows.

The better houses are grouped on the cross roads as if to take advantage of the clearer air. On the one side is the 'Bunch of Grapes,' on the other the stream, which used to drive the mill, dammed and deep behind a red wall, reflecting the coarse yellow reeds and the wooden warehouses. The water lies dark and full without vibration: it seems as if all the stillness in the neighbourhood were gathered into it. People stop and stare, their hands on the wall as if they were compelled; or they push open the iron wishing gate and stand looking at their own shining pause in the gathered depth.

Beyond the piece of waste ground are a few skinny willows, the contracted planes of the railway station and the winter sunrise.

Dollbright rented a narrow-fronted, three-storeyed house next to the mill yard. It ran a long way back through a disused scullery and bakehouse to a small courtyard of grass and stones, which was also approached by a private gated alley. High brick walls enclosed it on two sides, and on the third the back premises of another shabbier house which faced on Mill Street. In one corner of the courtyard was a steep flight of wooden steps leading to a cellar, and having a trap door which was suspended by a chain from a ring in the wall. The front of Dollbright's house, which was opposite a cigarette shop, showed bow windows stocked with plants and birdcages, a smooth doorstep, and a brass knocker shaped like a fan. He was a clerk in an ironmonger's shop. His employer possessed two businesses in Chepsford—one large and glass-fronted in the High Town, where he kept four assistants, and the other at Mill End which was more or less a rough and handy store. Dollbright worked at the latter; he and another man looked after everything. The ironmonger's name was John Bridges. He called in once or twice a week to have a look round the stock and the premises and examine the receipts. That was all. Bridges was one whom Dollbright regarded as being of monstrous spiritual outline. In fleshly looks he was rather handsome. He was living with another man's wife. She was beautiful, with arms and breasts like a young girl's in spite of her forty odd years, and heavy black unparted hair hiding her neck. Dollbright had seen them walking together in the town before they built their house in the country.

The lights in that house, he thought, shone like restless consciences. He imagined the childless couple full of acid regrets and disillusionment, tied in a dual solitude. It was a fact that nearly every window was lit up often all night through, seeming as if the place were burning through a shell.

Dollbright served John Bridges impersonally. His punishment would follow.

On Saturday mornings Bridges stopped his car outside the shop, walked in with his yellow muffler hanging outside his coat, pitched his hat on the desk and, scratching the back of his head, bawled in his loud voice:

'Morning, Dollbright. How's everything?' Then Dollbright

slid off his stool and showed him everything he wished to examine, meanwhile regarding him as sparsely as possible.

Once he was gone he never gave Bridges a look, not even if he had arrived in a new car or had another man waiting for him outside. He went back to his desk, dipped his steady pen in the ink and continued his work. He felt no throb at serving this man for whom he had nothing but a sure contempt. But after hearing Ifor Morriss's emphatic sermon, received without a protest in the church, the missing connection struck him absolutely for the first time, that such men as Bridges and this rotten parson were potent to work harm, to pull those of frail strength down beside their complacent length, to contaminate and loosen evil influences: that if it were in God to punish them eternally it was in man to curb them on earth. He was walking home and had covered half the distance. He paused. His violent denunciatory rage left him. He was quick to see the end which this enlarged vision indicated. He must give up his job; he knew it in a moment, but the thought flinched like flesh from flame, and he saw only Ifor Morriss's face, heard his voice strong as an echo, proclaiming his horrible phrase, 'God in the dock.'

On reaching Chepsford he turned down the back streets towards his home. They were empty and glistening. As he passed an alley the screeching of a woman ricocheted off the walls, and the roar of a man's cursing. Further on was a large window holding a lamp on the ledge inside. Contention pierced the ears with din, and peace was represented by a soundless light.

What chance had voiceless calm against the yell of common dispute? The world seemed to be screaming from its vents, jarring on its rusty poles, wounded and torn and wasted by naked outcry. 'Bloody… bloody… bloody,' rang on the stones.

The unnatural, unworn shapes of the gas works, the mill and the brewery cut into the yellowish haze of lighting which hung above the town. Directly sun, wind and rain bent their strength on these forged masses, men repaired and replaced them with sharp new outlines. They belonged to nothing but ingenuity, strange and disturbing idols which served human purposes as gods must serve. A steeple now was different; it might have been erected by the spirit. Yet the mill chimney pointed the same path and seemed grimed by efforts to attain it. Dollbright pursued his frequent invisible tracks along Mill Street. Here, with poor and patient living, is the frenzy which often kindles it to blazing catastrophe and death. Down those steps a maddened lorry driver flung his wife, breaking both her legs; from this door a brawl started which finished half a mile away with one man hammering another's skull upon the pavement; over this squalid pub, reeking, ill-lit, two brothers fought, and one died, for its possession.

Ha, what a town! What a vital, wicked, boisterous town, which beneath its vigorous life conceals a black current of despair and misery, and what people! Wild, vehement, laughing, whose two hands are generosity and vice, and whose eyes are weapons! There are none like them in all the rest of England, unbelievable as they are to these civil gentlemen in collars and—never mind. I speak the truth, but the gentlemen will not be convinced. It is enough if they can be led to see this secret and defended country, with its red fields flogged by the rain, its floods, storms in the elms, clouds tossed over the hills and dissolving in moonlight, wild moods of unleashed winds and pathetic stillnesses. If they can feel its power of height and valley. *I* am possessed with it. I see it night and day. Well, that's nothing. I am young and the gentlemen say that when I am older I shall learn better. I shall then write of a country and its quaint customs preening themselves in old-world nooks. That will please them, and I shall be enriched by their pedantic pleasure to such a degree of tin-wheeled liberty that the world itself will be no more to me than an unloved province, and belief shrink to the length of my sight—which is short.

*

When he was within a few yards of his own door Dollbright was stopped by a young man, who was standing on the edge of the pavement holding an unlighted cigarette.

'Got a match?'

Dollbright tersely signified that he had not.

'It's a fine lucky night for me,' the young man jeered, his eyebrows twitching.

'You can get a light over there; light enough to burn you,' Dollbright retorted, pointing at the 'Bunch of Grapes' whose half open door represented to him the crack of doom.

'I don't need that sort of light. My head's red hot already. God, this town is vile, and all the squalling, shouting people in it! What a Sunday night! It didn't start like this though.'

'Pull yourself together,' Dollbright snapped, and left him.

The young man gave his back a venomous glance, then slouched away with a kind of despondent sickliness, hiding the pale paring of his cheek in the collar of his coat. The world ignored his suffering; he spat on it for its lack of feeling. Dollbright and Mill End knew him as an aloof creature with a cruel tongue. His face seemed to swoop on the edge of their industrious existences like a haggard meteor. His name was Bellamy Williams, and he was a packer and grain handler. Dollbright entered his house through the back. His kitchen window was whitewashed over the lower half, but the clear panes showed the draughty flicker of a candle. Rain dripped into the water butt. Sitting on the fender was a man with a stiff beard and large fleshy-lobed ears, dressed in a shiny-backed waistcoat and black trousers to which were clinging wood shavings and traces of sawdust. He was polishing a brass clock face which he gripped between his knees. This was Benjamin Wandby, one of the two lodgers. The other was his sister.

'Hallo, you're late. Been far?'

'Yes,' said Dollbright gratingly.

He locked up and went to bed. His wife was asleep. Without waking her he lay down beside her and turning on his back, looked at the beam which ran straight across the ceiling. The street lamp shining through the bow window moulded it into a harsh wedge. On the stroke of the Market Hall clock the lamp went out, and in all the room there was no gleam save for one knob of the brass bed. Again and again he cursed the sermon he had heard, as if his over-tired brain were too numbed to relinquish its hold. He slept. But good God, how he dreamed and was locked by his dream!

It was of wagons with iron wheels all rolling towards the cattle market. Beneath nets palsied faces gaped at him and hands were crooked. A voice chanted: 'A wagon wheel with an iron rim, a wagon wheel with an iron rim, a wagon wheel with an iron rim.'

Then it was of Ifor Morriss, who gesticulated dumbly from

a pulpit raised up high in a soaring vault. His frightful scowl was directed like a ray upon Benjamin Wandby, John Bridges and his mistress; their faces, steeped in an evil pallor, floated towards his lips and hung—horror bubbling upon them as if he would dribble them down his blue chin. He waved his arms and shouted:

'I'm a chosen minister from the dark lake!'

And at once Dollbright saw the Dark Lake. The Gadarene swine hurled themselves into it, and were engulfed by an unbroken wave… .

He grasped his wife's shoulder.

'Eh? Frank, what's the matter? Let me strike a light?'

'Infernal demon,' he muttered.

She shivered with superstitious fear of the unconscious voice, and made an effort to wake him thoroughly. He sat up and wiped his forehead.

'I've had an awful dream. I saw a fiend preaching damnation. No, don't light the candle. I'm all right now. Oh, Florence!'

'You've got something on your mind?'

'Yes, I'll tell you.'

While he was going over the previous evening aloud they both heard a repeated muffled blow downstairs, and Florence said:

'It's Mr. Wandby hammering. Lately he's often been up all night.'

'Ah,' Dollbright agreed absently. He announced that he intended to leave Bridges. Florence was astounded. She started up in the bed.

'I'm sure you *must* be ill. How could we go on? We can't live and pay the rent out of what we get from the Wandbys.

Don't talk such wild nonsense. If you give up your job you won't find it easy to find another these days, and I shall have to keep you. It's wicked to think of such a thing when people all over Chepsford are fighting for work. We'll end up in the union.'

'It's no use talking like that, Florence. I've seen what I must do, and would be accursed to continue against my judgment. In time, perhaps, I shall be able to thank God that he sent me to hear that sermon.'

'That I won't, if it ends in you throwing away our living. When I married you my mother said: "He'll always look after you." Now lie down, and promise me you'll go on.'

'I thought you saw with me,' he cried.

'Because I kept silence while you talked?'

Those were the last words between them that night. At seven o'clock when it was still dark he descended into the clammy kitchen to light the fire. He was stuffing the grate with chips and shavings when she appeared in the doorway, grasping her dressing-gown on the breast.

'Do you still mean to give notice or were you feverish after a nightmare, Frank?'

'I mean to give notice the next time Mr. Bridges comes to the shop. I'm not going to write.'

'Are you going to tell him why?'

'I don't know.'

'I thought not.'

'Oh, Florence, don't taunt me!'

She seized his wrist in her hard fingers and stared at him, her face streaky with anger.

'Listen to me, Frank. If you give notice you'll be nothing but a selfish stuck-up prig. I know you too well to think you're

what other folk'll call you—and that's a lazy improvident
husband. So far you've taken good care of me, although I was
below you when you married me and used to toiling. But now
I haven't the strength to go on if you throw all the load on me.
And I can't see any connection between Mr. Morriss's sermon
and working for John Bridges where you've been for fifteen
years and well treated. You just remember that what's easy to
come by in youth is out of reach in old age. It's a mad idea, or
a cracked false idol of a religion that makes you drive your
wife silly with worry and let everything get uncertain at our
time of life. If you think Mr. Bridges'll mind your opinion of
what he thinks fit to do, you'll find you're wrong. Listen: if
he told you to go through some ridiculous notion of what God
ought to mean to you, and you'd done well at your job, you'd
never get over such mean treatment. He won't think so much
of you though; he's rich and can get a dozen clerks in your
place, but you'll find you only fit one stool! You think
everybody should shun him. You'd like to see him an outcast.
Well, you won't. And what the Lord thinks of John Bridges
he's thought already. It's madness … madness, and it's not
fair on me. I'm fifty, and I go on and on with people I don't
care about; yet you'll put me aside for a notion that knocked
you over in a night.'

'Florence,' he said earnestly, taking her hand, 'how can you
use such arguments to me? You know I'll look after you. And
you know I must do what I think is right, or how can I endure
myself? This Mr. Morriss said his "faith" was broad to live
by, and I think mine was the same; such men as Bridges are
dangerous as contagious diseases. Let him get his new clerk,
for I'll have nothing more to do with him. His life is a
reflection of what goes on within him, and my working for

him was a reflection of a slack conscience. My mind's made up.'

'Very well,' she finished and went away; it was not the end: until the next Saturday she opposed his decision with bitter obstinacy and he began to question himself as to the real soul of this stiff hard-working woman. She was a devout member of the Baptist chapel, and her opposition took the shape henceforward of a warning against spiritual pride. Yet, through the chinks of a self-righteous anger, he seemed to see a secret contempt. Had she been hoarding resentment against him for years? Her wrath appeared of no new birth, but fully formed and skilful in attack. He could not put the sight of it from his mind. Rage shrivelled her lips and lit an icy green spark in her eyes. He felt an actual pain in his chest as if part of him had been torn away. At times it was no less than agony, even after he had been praying. Once, when she was asleep and he beside the bed which he had left, upon his knees, in a paroxysm of grief, he furtively reached for her relaxed hand and pressed it urgently upon the spot over his heart, cherishing himself with his wife rather than with the image of his God. The flesh called to him with consolation and with peace. With temptation, too, as he understood it. He whispered, 'Florence,' but was too divided to recall her, and laid her hand again at her side in hollow silence.

II

A COMMERCIAL traveller stayed the night in Chepsford at the 'George,' and was late in starting the next morning. He was driving too fast to leave a margin of safety for rash children, and just after turning the corner of Mill Street into the cross roads, he was unable to avoid a little girl. She was knocked down just outside the Mill yard. A neighbour of the Dollbrights', a young woman named Menna Trouncer, was passing, and seeing the empty car standing still in the middle of the road, asked one of the crowd, which had gathered, what had happened.

'I was just asking,' was all the answer given, and not being morbidly inquisitive, Menna was about to go home, when she happened to lookup; in the tallet from which the lorries were loaded, Bellamy Williams was leaning, his arms hanging forward and his head thrown back, as if he were filling his lungs with the drizzly air. She did not know if he caught sight of her, but he suddenly retreated. In another moment Menna had run into the packing room. Machinery seemed to rumble in the dusty rafters, and two men powdered with meal were rolling trolleys over the white floor which reverberated under the iron wheels. In the thick moted atmosphere a fine pollen was visible which softened the ticket rollers and the men's faces and shirts to chalky hues. The bloated sacks, of a feeble pallor, were behind Bellamy. He had covered his face. With his shoulders heaving he was retching dryly.

'Here, give it to me,' she said to a nervous-looking boy, who was bringing a glass of water. He surrendered it, relieved.

'Drink this, Bellamy.'

He took it from her and swallowed it all. Then he could speak.

'Thank you. *You*, Menna; what're you doing here?'

'I saw you through the tallet.'

'Why the devil was I made so squeamish?'

'I suppose you saw the accident?'

'Yes, the whole of it. Foh—'

His mouth shuddered: 'Don't go thinking I mind you seeing what a sickly anaemic spirit I have—it's having to bear it that maddens me.'

He glanced at his clenched hands: 'You must get out, Menna, or the manager will be sending to find out what the trouble is.'

'I'm going.'

From his lips, pressed into angry endurance, broke the words, low and threatening:

'I *will* have you. You could love me and you shall.'

She restrained herself from touching him, but as she walked away, without looking at him, she was conscious of him in the corner of her sight, idle, gathering strength to force his will.

'He'll say I lead him on, then refuse him,' she thought. 'I don't care—anybody that knew him would have gone up to see if he were ill. He'll say what's nastiest anyway. He *did* say the other night he didn't mind what happened to me or how much I suffered as long as I loved him. That's what they all seem to think of me; they can talk nicely to their other girls and I'm the one to comfort them. I won't have it…I won't pity him … why should he think I'll be good to him?'

She turned round, marched back to the mill, and, stopping under the tallet, shouted Bellamy's name.

'Hallo,' he said, approaching, and standing like a cast newly unpacked from bran.

'Will you come and see me to-night?'

He dropped a muffled 'Of course I will.'

She instantly disappeared behind the wall, reappearing in the distance, her head bare and defiant. She had forgotten that she was still carrying the empty glass until a voice asked her:

'Why don't you fill it, Miss?'

The glass came from the 'Bunch of Grapes;' she knew the shape. So she went in. The bar was empty, except for a man in overalls who was writing something on the margin of a newspaper, and a gross woman with a glazed face and bilious eyes, whose head was tilted against the wall a couple of inches below a sort of framed mourning card which read:

'POOR TRUST IS DEAD.'

The man was a stranger: the woman was her mother.

'Get back an' mind the shop, Menna.'

She silently took the key held out to her, stuck out her lower lip in disgust, and leaving the glass on the counter, ran home.

It was this Mrs. Trouncer whom Dollbright particularly regarded as a deformed soul which would ultimately be cast out: it was from her that he had drawn his picture of the evil liver.

She was the widow of a Salus man, which town she had left on his death eighteen months before, and already she was famous in Mill End as a drinker who outdid most men when she was in the way of it. By trade she was a dealer in second-hand clothes.

Her appearance filled him with an extreme, almost

superstitious, horror. She was very much like a mottled toad without the beautiful eyes. Her breath was dank as if her lungs were marsh plants. In dress she was sombrely respectable; her bulk leant dignity to voluminousness. She and her daughter Menna lived in the old house at the other end of his alley.

Work ceased at the mill at five o clock. Bellamy Williams changed his coat and before six was on the threshold of the shop, looking through the small-paned window which was green in the corners, to see if Menna were there. Across a row of shoes and between a red hat and a silver sequined dress, he saw her drooping profile. He went in. On the counter was a heap of black drapery which seemed to absorb most of the lamplight. A woman, staggeringly fat, with oily hair, was standing with her back to the door holding out a dark coat at both arms' length across herself, so that it looked like a theatre curtain swinging at the hem.

'The best mother that ever was,' she was saying mournfully.

While the sale was continuing, Bellamy stared at Menna. Her hair, which just touched her shoulders, made him think of a spread sheaf on the ground.

She got rid of the customer as soon as she could, though the woman saw fit to drop a tear or two on the threshold; Bellamy mocked her:

'She's so pleased with her trouble. See her twirling her skirts? There's the funeral to look forward to.'

He followed her into the kitchen. An iron pipe carried the smoke from the stove through a hole in the wall. A red cushion was squeezed as if by the pressure of a heavy bulk, into the crack of an old velveteen arm-chair.

Bellamy sat down, his clenched hands on his knees. His eyes stared like two blue worlds hanging in joyless space, dead and unrolling. Presently he leant forward and covered his face.

'Why don't you leave me alone? Why did you ask me here tonight when you know I melt at the sight of you?'

She retorted: 'Why do you nurse such a spite against me?'

'Because you could love me if you'd let yourself. You do already. But you lie to me, like all the others that live on lies. They tell half a lie and expect you to tell the other half. And if you won't you soon feel their mean little teeth. I can't cut myself off from the truth when I see it, but you can. You're worse than most: you have something real to give and you won't.'

She was picking at a splinter in the table.

'I haven't lied to you. You can't expect to understand the truth if you bang the door on it.'

'Menna, I can't bear to look at you when you say you don't love me. That's why I rushed away last Sunday. You do.'

'It's not so easy to say what I feel. Only a moment ago you told me I had something *to give*. That's what they all think. Nobody has anything to offer me.'

He sank with despair.

'I can't escape from hunger. And I can't help wanting to be fed.'

'Suppose I want to be fed too? Nobody thinks of that. I'm always the one to be sorry. Other girls have the right to enjoy themselves, and men don't hate them for it. Hate me if you like—that's why I wanted you to come back, so that you can see how little I care for blame.'

Bellamy flung her a look, furious, pitiful, baffled.

'That's it? Oh—'

He sprang up and backed against the wall as if to be shot.

'Here I am!' he cried loudly. 'What do you think of me? Don't I do you honour? Won't the girls envy you my broad shoulders and mealy cheeks? I'm as pale as a sack and as hefty as a wet label. I was sick this morning because I saw a child hurt. But I tell you, you can play with a madman less dangerously than with me. I've not been brought up in gentle tolerance of women's "Good boy, come here," and "Bad boy, go there." I've not been brought up at all: I've had my face scraped along a gritty road. I'll poison your vanity and you'll pity me and pity me until you have no rest, but cry out to love me, because your sight is sore. I adore you, and I hate you too. For twenty-two years I've searched for you. I won't give you up … you're mine!' She had moved the lamp; as she held it, like her own fixed glance it glared into his wild eyes, and his fanatical shadow bolted before him to the door where it hung suspended like a cloak.

'Arrange it as you wish—that's how it will be!' he shouted. She started towards him holding out her hand in stricken eagerness, but as he did the last time, he banged the door between them. And he thought: 'It's not enough to die. I'd like to bury my own body.'

All over in a moment, the sight of her! On the counter a candle with a long crooked wick was burning. A thread of greasy smoke flew from the flame. He blew it out.

'Now, why did I do that?'

He stepped into the street clutching his coat inside the pockets. He reeled in a gust of wind.

Menna carried the lamp upstairs. On her bed, in the dark, Mrs. Trouncer was lying with crossed feet, in a ghastly stupor. Filled like a bloated sponge she was less asleep than steeped in reeking fumes. The sparks of consciousness exploded, madly amazed, fiery atoms too feeble to bring reason to the dizzy senses. To-morrow she would lie there still, puffing out her lips and tugging at her ears, her yellow gaze fixed on her ultimate terror—death.

Menna took away the matches. From her room she heard the moans and sea whispers which continued all the night. It was a house of awful sights and shades which might stain the walls with the filmy silhouettes of appalling postures and deathly collapses.

*

Saturday, Florence Dollbright watched her husband walk away from the house and then complained to the charwoman about the way she was washing the passage. The charwoman, kneeling on a mat with her skirts slumping over her heels, looked up as if she did not know what to do next. Then she hurriedly shuffled her hands in the bucket of grey water and squeezing out the house-flannel, wiped every crack between the stones until no traces of suds were left.

'You, viper … what's up with you?' she muttered.

The pavements looked as if she had been washing them and had swilled the water into the gutters. It was raining, a dull, dirty winter rain.

Florence went across the street to the cigarette shop. The living room was at the back. Her friend, Mrs. Emily Jones, was dishevelled, and one string of her blue apron was undone. She hugged her bosom and kissed Florence, telling her that they were all in a muddle and she wasn't to notice them. Through the crack of an inner door Mr. Jones' arm in a white shirt sleeve could be seen moving as he shaved. He was barman at the 'Bunch of Grapes.'

'I've got a headache, Freda's got a bad tooth, and Dad's full of argument,' said Mrs. Jones.

Freda, a plump girl with a spotty neck, who had been looking at herself in a glass with 'Players' Navy Cut,' inscribed on it, turned round and tried to conceal her swollen face.

'She won't go to the dentist,' continued Mrs. Jones.

'Oh Mam, shut up!'

'Well then go away and don't talk about how it hurts.'

Florence begged her friend to come home with her for a few minutes. She particularly wanted to see her, she said earnestly. The marks of tears had softened her piercing eyes.

Mrs. Jones, in her husband's coat, ran with Florence to the Dollbrights' house. They went up to the bedroom where, to her surprise, a fire was burning. Florence banged the window. Her hand was lying on her breast.

'Emily I don't want you to tell anybody,' she pulled down her dress.

'My good God, you haven't found anything there!'

Florence nodded feebly. Her hands would settle on the venomous centre of her fear. This was the first step towards finding out. She thought of a white, cold, hospital ward.

'When I was combing my hair I happened to touch myself. That was a fortnight ago. I thought perhaps I'd strained a muscle and the lump would go down; I've rubbed it with embrocation and rested my arm as much as possible but it's still there.'

Her voice was thin, her lips pressed together. 'Does it hurt you?'

'No.'

'Have you told Francis?'

'No … no. Not yet.'

She knelt in front of Emily, and took her by the wrist.

'Feel there. You can press your hand in. I never feel any pain.'

Emily pressed her fingers into the undercurve of the breast. Beneath the flesh she felt a hard, seemingly movable substance. She gave an hysterical sob, and hid her face in Florence's shoulder. She was now calm, with blue shadows round her mouth. Her reflection in the tilted mirror seemed to be musing.

'Hush,' she said.

Emily cried:

'Haven't you been to the doctor?'

'No.'

'But you must! You must go. It may be one of those ordinary lumps. I forget what they're called, but Tom's mother had one, and the doctor said 'twas nothing to be afraid of: you can't put a name to it by yourself, Florrie. We're ignorant.'

'I know what this is called.' Florence said violently, as if in a spasm. 'This is called *cancer*.'

'Oh, my good God, don't say that! You've no call to say that yet, Florrie. And even if it is, maybe if you take it in time, it'll never come back. It'll come out like a weed.'

'Leaving the roots. To think of such a bitter, ugly thing hiding here, *here*, eating my life out. Like a worm eating me, as if I were dead. Ah the hideous thing,' Florence wailed, covering her breast.

'Florrie, Florrie, don't!'

'Frank doesn't guess what's under here. When he lies down beside me he doesn't know the worm that never sleeps. It's come to me. My mother died of it. Oh, if I could tear it and burn it, tear it and burn it, tear it and burn it!'

She raised her clenched fists; deliriously she hit and clawed herself. Her mouth was torn by a fearful grimace. Emily, white lipped and terrified, ran screaming for help.

Florence was given sal volatile and put to bed. Emily, and Margaret Wandby, Benjamin's sister, sat beside her until she was quiet. The latter, a bewildered-looking old maid, kept bending her head and gazing into the pupils of Florence's red eyes. They asked if they should send for her husband.

'No, let him come home and find what he's done with his fine religious pride. Let him see for himself when he's finished showing God: don't stop him when he comes in. Don't tell him.' She stared at the cobweb she had meant to brush away.

'Let it stay,' she moaned, without knowing, what she meant: 'let it stay, let it stay.'

*

John Bridges' ironmongery at Mill End was only part of an old wooden building and consisted of one room on the ground floor, from which a ladder led to one above through an opening in the plank ceiling. It faced the blank wall of a cooperative warehouse on the opposite side of the road. Posters were stuck there every week by an old man with a yellow moustache, who somehow made one think of a Viking. To the right was an iron wishing gate, giving entrance to a path along the stream called the Rats' Ramble by the people of Mill End, and Willow Walk by town councillors.

The same customers appeared regularly; the same faces sailed across the window on the way to work and back. The Viking shouted from the top of his steps, trains whistled, lorries loaded with planks and sacks of grain splashed mud on the dusty panes.

The assistant was a spindle-limbed man whose sorrel-coloured hair hung over his forehead. He seemed to have no stomach, but swinging across the cavity was a huge steel watch chain. He wore a drab linen coat, and his figure suited and mingled with the dull light in the shop. His name was Williams. He was the father of Bellamy.

When Bellamy came into the shop, as he often did, straight from the mill, in a dusty shirt, old Williams would say: 'Here comes my floury baby,' and Bellamy shot a malevolent glance at his sardonic old father. For the shamed consciousness that he had never been anybody's baby was Bellamy's greatest trouble.

Old Williams had been married twice, and of his wives had only this one son, the child of the second. She died a month after his birth, and Bellamy was reared by a policeman's wife. He had lived with her ever since.

There's not much to be added to old Williams's portrait. His habits were inflexible. He always sat either at the top or bottom of the ladder; in his spare time he made hard leather gloves, sewing the seams together with large crooked black stitches like spiders' legs.

He had been working for Bridges even longer than Dollbright, to whom he had confided his whole history from his birth. This prolonged anecdote took several days. After it was finished he spoke seldom to his companion, but stitched and mumbled to himself.

One day Dollbright overheard a few words which impressed him. They were about a minister who had preached, Williams muttered to himself, with the 'brimming authority of sin.'

Dollbright was near to breaking down from his incessant pondering on the responsibilities of the righteous. His mind was confused, but fearfully active, and every sense drained into his fanatical conscience. Poor wretch, he loved his flinty God, who came at him like a hammer.

*

His desk at the ironmongery was a sort of boxed-in affair; it was high, with a stool and a crude electric light, whose white shade resembled a tilted face. A telephone of an obsolete and clumsy pattern was attached to the wall between suspended files of letters and receipts.

On Saturday morning, at the usual time of eleven o'clock, John Bridges' car stopped outside the shop. Out got Bridges well wrapped up in muffler and brown overcoat, and in he walked cheerfully shouting:

'Morning both of you. How's everything?' Flop went his hat on the desk. Williams descended saying, as he always did:

'Quiet, sir.'

And Dollbright rising from the desk, replied: 'All right, sir.'

Bridges was quick. He made a few enquiries about sales, then prepared to take himself off, remarking:

'Well, it's cold; and I want a livener.'

Happening to glance carelessly enough at Dollbright he stopped near the door and asked:

'Anything up?'

'I'd like to give notice, sir.'

Bridges nearly flung his hat on the floor. Going close to Dollbright, so that the other could see his eyes glaring with angry surprise, he repeated loudly:

'*You* … you want to give notice? You want to leave here? What the devil's up with you?'

'I want to give notice.'

Bridges' face plunged towards him. He suddenly lost his temper.

'Very well then, I accept it. At the end of the week—'

Deeply vexed he swung round and walked out of the shop. As he was getting into the car he hesitated. It was unusual for him, but he valued Dollbright. Perhaps something had gone wrong.

He re-entered and found the two men standing exactly where he had left them as if they were waxworks.

'Come out here,' he said to Dollbright who followed him into the road. They walked a few steps in the rain. Grey rags of newspapers blew along the gutter and thick white smoke, like a silent explosion, burst from the station. Standing still, with his hands in his pockets, Bridges scrutinized his clerk.

'You've been very abrupt. You worked for my father before the business was made over to me, and you know even better than I do what we can sell. I can't think that this is an ordinary occurrence. Has anything happened to you?'

'Yes, sir: the only way is to go.'

'I should like to know why. Are you dissatisfied with anything?'

'With my employer.'

'Up there is the Labour Exchange. I was there this morning. Your reasons must be strong. But, Dollbright, you're imagining them … you're on the brink of a dream. You look overwrought. I'm half suspicious, though not so far as I'm lost. Tell me plainly what you mean.'

'Plainly is best. I don't care to work for you any more, because I abominate your way of living.'

Bridges was infuriated. Tautly he extracted his pocket book; with a cutting directness he handed Dollbright his wages.

'You God-forgotten swine, blast your holy insolence. Go to the devil and don't come back.' He shut his teeth, sprang into the car, stamped it into speed, and was gone. Dollbright was left holding his money, and dully wondering how he came to be grieving over the very wheelmarks in the mud.

He returned to fetch his hat and coat. He put them on—the same stiff mackintosh and the same black hat. He closed the ledger. If not his morals, at least something of Bridges and of himself was in the figures… .

Williams raised his voice:

'Where are you off to?'

'I'm going.'

'You've never had a row with the boss?'

Dollbright nodded: 'I'm going for good.'

'You fool! You blame fool!' Williams shouted. 'Now what am I to do?' he burst out in a torrent of words: 'there's no peace. There'll be 'undreds of clever-daisy fellows comin' in to see if the stool fits them and the desk's low enough for their bloody elbows. They'll tear me to shreds with their questions … it'll all fall on me. Then I shall smash their glasses for 'em, and it'll be the Union for me along with all the lousy scamps that Mill End's shut of. And that's the *best*, and may be weeks to come. But what's to be done now? Who the hell is going to carry on with your work? Have I got to do it all?'

'Comfort yourself,' said Dollbright, in a terse vision of the future, 'it'll all be done smoothly. Good-bye.'

He was right. Half an hour after his departure Bridges rang up.

'That you, Williams? Good. Can you hang on by yourself

until Monday? I've got someone coming. No, never mind the books. That's all right then. So long.'

Dollbright went home by an unaccustomed way. The street was narrow, like a cañon cleft in sulphur-coloured brick; it was sickly with the smell of boiling from the brewery. Rows of gloomy incavated windows stared straight into their opposites. A yellow lorry leaning in the gutter cast a reflection on the wet asphalt.

The street took him two minutes to walk from end to end. His face was like a wrestler's, twisted with effort. Could he go to Bridges, apologize, and use sick nerves as an excuse? Why did not God tempt with devils?

'Devils I could resist, but thou temptest me with my wife, and the very image of right.'

His meditation was too fierce to be prayerful.

He emerged on Market Hill. From there the roofs of Mill End are visible as an uneven floor of slate, cracked across and across with irregular dark lines. Like a single streak of indestructible rock the mill chimney leaps above the plateau daring a rarer light... .

Men feel their gods on heights, clutch them as if by the ankle, and pray to the soaring intelligence. Dollbright's eyes flew across the drop to the stern summit.

'An army—and no army of men—has charged me. Thou hast made thyself plain. While my blood beats I will continue, or let the wind put out my pulse. Thou leadest us all: lead my soul in prayer to thee. Thou art God, I believe it, I believe it.'

People noticed him. He lowered his head and returned home.

The first person he saw was Mrs. Jones, holding a tumbler in her hand with the obvious yet indefinable air of attendance on the sick. He looked her up and down in astonishment. She sometimes called him 'sir,' and was always prouder of being Florence's friend when she was speaking to him. She fumbled with the loose apron string.

'Is anything the matter, Mrs. Jones?'

'Oh, I thought p'raps someone had sent for you. She's gone to sleep. I've been sitting with her. You don't want to worry, Mr. Dollbright.'

'Florence?' he stammered.

'She was a bit upset and hysterical after you'd gone out.'

'Thank you,' he said. He walked softly into their room. His wife was sunken on the bed, her cheek-bones streaked with colour. Her sleep was almost soundless. The alarm clock ticked under the eiderdown.

He stretched his hands towards her feet without touching them.

'Thou art God. I believe it. Amen, Amen, Amen.'

An hour later she awoke and saw him near the window. He heard her turn her head and looked at her slowly.

'Well, have you done it?' She threw at him.

'Yes.'

'Then leave me alone. I don't want to see you.'

Holding up her thin hard fingers she laughed scathingly.

*

That evening the baggy figure of Benjamin Wandby was to be seen parading The Rats' Ramble. He walked the whole length of it some five or six times, gazing absently at the occasional passers.

'There's no doubt about it,' he said to himself, and a few

steps further on, repeating the words in an undertone, he continued: 'The world was never peopled with beauty. In fact the whole scheme was probably a great deal uglier than it is now. Flawed from the beginning. And so is each individual.'

He sat down near the lock gate, noticing how the mud oozed round the sides of his boots among the prints of many feet.

'I wonder if Menna will marry young Wlliams. Her nature is curious, very *very* curious—almost like a relaxing climate. He's just the man to attract her. She pities him; but would she pity him if he didn't want her, or if he were old and repulsive? No. Lovers' sympathy only, and when he's taken it there'll be none left for ordinary life. A woman isn't created for one man; but certainly for one kind—if there's any distinction.' The five o'clock train whistled in the distance, approached, ran on the bridge, and rushed behind the willows. Benjamin saw the tormented glare of fire among the drizzly branches; he felt the seat shake, and the shock in the ground. He turned and stared up at the grey iron plates welded with mighty rivets, to which drops of water were clinging. The stone coping twinkled like granite. For some reason it cleaned every thought out of his head. Besides, he saw that he was being watched from a window of the railway hotel. He got up and moved away. For two hours he occupied himself in taking to pieces an admirable copy of a Dresden china clock, which he had bought in the market for ten shillings. Sometimes he stopped; a listless expression came into his eyes and he let his idle hands lie on the table in front of him.

Heaven only knows why he looked so sad. It was the coming of old age perhaps…

Mrs. Jones used to remark to Florence: 'That Mr. Wandby

of yours looks sad, don't you think. He must have been through some trouble.'

'Oh I don't think so …I hadn't noticed.'

'I daresay he was crossed in love.' Mrs Jones ascribed all shades of melancholy to this crimson affliction. Men and women alike were all sufferers, it was the universal blow, and apparently incurable. Grandfathers and grandmothers had been crossed in love and, in spite ot rearing intervening families, had never recovered.

One of Benjamin's peculiarities was very apparent in his room; he never put anything in drawers or cupboards. He kept the bulk of his clothes in piles on chairs, and hung the smaller pieces, like socks and ties, over the end of the bed, but that doesn't matter much; it has no bearing on his future. If you begin a man's history at sixty, it's best to take all the details for granted. He has acquired so many.

At supper, which Dollbright and the Wandbys ate together, Florence being still in bed, he seemed bent on ineptitude. His place was at the bottom of the table next to the lamp, which shone on his glowing ear and made his beard look like fine wire.

'When I was a boy I used to walk on stilts,' said he, 'not the ordinary foot or foot-and-a-half stilts but proper ones, a yard high. I had a long pair of cotton trousers to cover them, and a top hat. Then I'd rub flour on my face and walk up and down the village street peering into the second-floor windows. People were very angry because they never heard me coming; even when I was watching them they didn't always see me. I was a lad on those stilts, I can tell you! I saw plenty of queer things.'

'He talks like an idiotic child,' Dollbright thought impatiently. He was staring out of the window at the stab of light thrown by the street lamp. It was not immediately under it, but some distance away, jagged and detached. The black shadows of a couple standing under the post were not long enough to touch it. A wet night, shining like tar…

'I remember a queer old chap who used to live in a large house at the bottom of the town—a squire or something. A Mr. What's-his-name, a gentleman anyway. Funny I should remember him so well! Everybody was afraid of him, so, of course, they talked about him. The girls that worked there— the maids that is—said he wouldn't allow anyone into his room, not even to peep round the door. But I saw into that room; I looked in at the window, and there he was sitting on the side of the bed with a weather glass on his knee, like this, holding it like a banjo, it was summer, just before dusk, when the sun's gone and the mosquitoes begin to bite your neck. There was a row of old lime trees in of that house; they threw such a queer green shade on the wall behind that old man! I can see it now. I can see his whiskers and his white knuckles, and the wrinkled bed under a dirty quilt. I was a fool. Instead of staying quiet, I must go and shout out: "Thang, twang! give us a song, mister," and what do you think he did?'

'I don't know,' said Margaret, astonished.

'Ha… well, he heaved that barometer right through the glass, straight at me. Lord didn't I run! For weeks after I kept out of his way in case he got hold of me and gave me a thrashing.'

He got up and went to the fire. Margaret sat chafing the backs of her yellow hands, bending her head a little to the left, her eyes vacant. Her dress, grey in the light, deepened to black near the floor. She had always a dry line along her lips. Dollbright still watched the figures beneath the lamp-post. They were Menna's and Bellamy Williams'.

The motionless bird-cage hung in the window, covered with a cloth which hid the silent birds. The tall geraniums grew dimly.

'I wonder if we shall remember *this* room,' said Benjamin.

'We shall not have time. We are all getting old. It's only time that sorts out memories.'

Both were startled by Dollbright's harsh tone.

'Talking of stilts has put an idea into my head,' Benjamin remarked. He stretched out his legs.

'Look what an uncomfortable shape man is. He can't twine himself round a support; he can't cuddle himself and keep warm when he's getting old because of *this*?'

He touched his body.

'It's stiff, it's awkward. It gets in the way, it gets cramp and dyspepsia. Now if man were all leg, right up to the neck, think how we could tie ourselves into warm knots for the night. Think how we could run and leap! Though I suppose it wouldn't be much of an improvement; our legs would glide apart and we should collapse like clumsy skaters— '

'Benjamin, are you going to do any work tonight?'

'Presently.'

He looked at Dollbright.

'Didn't you go to hear Ifor Morriss preach last week?'

'I did.'

'I was told something about him. They say he takes the collection money for himself. Steals it in fact. And goes to the service in bedroom shoes.'

'I don't want to hear anything about Ifor Morriss,' said Dollbright. Indeed the name rang in his head like a demon bell. He went out of the door. Benjamin's eyes followed him. Then the sister and brother exchanged a long enigmatic scrutiny.

'I think a long way back,' said he.

She bent her head and quietly rubbed her hands while the dirty plates remained on the table.

Again that night Benjamin and Dollbright talked. They were in the kitchen, alone.

Benjamin stood in his dressing gown, his neck bare.

'There's a clerk wanted in Jagg's yard. You might get the place if you go round to-morrow.'

'Who told you I wanted work?' cried Dollbright fiercely.

'Young Williams. And whether you want it or not, I think you're going to need it soon. Try for it. You've got to think of Florence.'

'*Florence*? Since when have you called my wife by her Christian name?'

Wandby put his hand on Dollbright's shoulder.

'Take your damned paw off me!' He started upright and swiped his open hand across Wandby's cheek, leaving a thick red flush. Wandby leapt back against a chair which fell over sideways.

'That's how I've thought of you,' he burst out in a throttled agonized voice, 'that's how I've met you before, Dollbright, long, long before I ever saw you. You're cruel … I saw cruelty in your eyes. That can't be hidden from me. I know human faces to the bone—to the brain, to the soul. You're a judge. Be my judge.'

Holding his cheek he stumbled out, his sidelong and terrified stare clinging to Dollbright as if in anticipation of a second blow.

Dollbright noticed nothing after the fervent contact. He leant against the wall, panting, feeling the knot of his tie with smarting fingers. He shuddered: 'Ugh, what a vile touch. His beard touched my ear. Ugh, how beastly!'

*

For Menna and Bellamy the evening had been another of their poignant failures. They could not bear to part so, but it was half-past ten, and nothing but desperation came of being together.

They stood in the shop. The door moving to and fro by an inch, jarred on the latch. The moment was horribly painful.

'Are you coming to see me on Wednesday?' she asked.

'You know I can't keep away!' he exclaimed bitterly.

She broke away from his arm. As she shut the door after him he craved to knock, to make her open and pursue her, crying:

'Oh, Menna, Menna, Menna, don't leave me. Don't leave me like this. You have something I want that nobody else can give me. Comfort me. Oh, don't leave me—'

He ran home, undressed, and in his trouble sat naked in the dark, pressing his pyjamas to his eyes, covering his forehead. He felt as though he had lost everything. His heart was like a burden.

III

AN INVITATION to the gentlemen to leave sordid brutal Mill End for a moment and go with me up to Lindenfield, the wealthy residential district of Chepsford, where fighting is confined to lap dogs and cats, and rows are purely psychological.

Now for some style! A breath of it, so to speak, between ordinary inhaling. Are we all here? Or has someone encountered a mote too cumbersome for his windpipe and passed out on the way up White Cross Street? If one has, let him lie. Lindenfield, those acres of prosperity. That lighter side.

It's only fair that I should allot it a few words of description, if only to balance the less elegant half of Chepsford, where most of my characters lived and slogged. Lindenfield does not lack height—it is built on it; and most of the houses run to bell towers, minarets, glass observatories and other fancy devices. The gardens are evenly planted with flowering trees, which at this season were only exotic skeletons. Glossy laurels, and key-pattern walls ensure seclusion for sixty-two spinsters from five bachelors… In Lindenfield, at this time— (a few years back) lived an Irish doctor of whom I have written before. His house was a melancholy building, square, brown and severe, with a white gate. Of the doctor himself there is now nothing more to be said than that he was kind and generous and fond of a joke, if he made it.

He had, however, a rather grave face. It was so as he sat at his desk in the surgery while Florence Dollbright put on her hat. He noticed that she did not look in the mirror.

'Remember, it's essential; ye must have an operation.'

Papers were pushed aside. The ash tray was full of cigarette ends. The doctor was leaning back in his chair, his hands resting on his deeply wrinkled waistcoat.

Florence moved nervously, fastening up an end of hair at the back of her head. A high colour flamed on her cheek-bones, which made her appear distressed and awkward. She was at a disadvantage before his authority.

He, on his part, was observing her narrowly, particularly her hands. The wedding ring looked as if it had grown with her finger. The joints were swollen, the nails broken, the palm lined.

'Will it be very expensive?' she asked.

'Ye mustn't worry about that. It has to be done.'

'I can't help it…oh no, I don't worry now. I must get some one in to help,' she said, excited and vague, while successive flushes coloured her face a deeper and deeper red.

He opened the door and inclined his head as she passed him. Voices came down the passage from the panel patients' room, in busy and cheerful conversation:

'Oh no, it were summat wrong with 'is kidneys— '

'That's a poor look-out with six kids!'

'Come along,' the doctor called.

Florence thanked God she had no children, lest *this* should be running in their veins. It didn't mean much to anybody but herself. She thought vindictively of her husband, as if her illness were a punishment to him.

She stood on the wet doorstep, opening her umbrella. There was a question she had not asked: would the operation be terribly painful? In that house pain seemed a matter of course, and she had been afraid of being foolish. And why hadn't she told him her husband was out of work? The truth was she was ashamed. She had always been proud that he had looked after her so well—she had boasted of it.

Then the horror of certainty came over her again, and oblivious of everything but fear she hurried home. The beat of her rapid footsteps died away along the road, and the may tree dripped into the puddle under the gate.

Meanwhile, Dollbright was making his way to Jagg's timberyard, ignorant of all this. He went along the Rats' Ramble, beside the stream. It was olive green. Ducks were diving under the far bank, and a couple were dawdling to watch them. Behind him the shapes of the warehouses were already obscure. He heard the market hall clock strike five as he entered the yard. Near the gates an old dog looked at him droopingly from opaque eyes. A sign like an arch over the entrance read:

James Jagg and Son, Timber Merchants.

In the yard were heaps of raw logs, mostly elm, whole lopped trunks shrunken from the rough grey bark, and new planks under a shelter. The ground was slimy under a covering of cinders. In a corner was an idle steam engine.

It was a place of horizontal shadows. The office was a single room with red brick walls, and a sash window facing the road. Someone turned on the light, and the yard was lonelier than before.

Dollbright knocked at the door. Inside two men were talking and laughing. One of them was hooting like an owl. Dollbright first saw a man's shape on the glass panels, then the man himself, straightening a smile as he poked his head into the opening. He wore a hat and an overcoat, as if he were just going out.

'Good afternoon,' he said with a Welsh accent, 'what can I do for you?'

And even his thin crooked nose looked contemptuous and irritable; it was half day; he had been enjoying a rowdy talk.

'I want to see the manager.'

'He's gone to Clystowe,' the other voice remarked, scarcely clear for sniggering. As if to let it out, the first man opened the door wider, blocking it with his foot and rubbing his eye under the spectacles. He stood leaning his weight on the knob, a scraggy, lumpy, bony creature, sprouting moles on his greasy chin.

'Gone to Clystowe,' he repeated. 'So that's not much good, is it?'

'I don't know about that. Perhaps you can tell me what I want to know,' said Dollbright.

'Oh come on in; and shut the door; it's cold,' groused the inner voice.

Dollbright found himself in a little square room with a shabby desk, reeking of Turkish cigarettes, and in the company of two ugly men, who were winking at each other. He was immediately cast from hope of work by the disagreeable and mocking faces which confronted him. He was not daunted by their insolent security, but made certain of failure. The man who had let him in sneered at him aslant his nose; about the other there was a stunted look, as if he had been blasted in full growth, and his lip hung loosely beneath the moustache.

Dollbright persisted, nevertheless.

'I heard a clerk was wanted here.'

'You're too late. *He's* got in, and does fine.'

The man at the desk bit his lips, smiled and bowed himself from the waist towards Dollbright. Now it was his turn:

'Not so fast, wait a tick. You should have referred our friend to me. Which is boss here of us two?'

The man with the moles was very much amused, because neither was.

'Oh, you of course; you have the say,' he granted, sitting on the edge of the desk and fitting his hat on his knee, while he brushed the brim with the edge of his cuff.

'You must listen to him. You see?' he wound up, grinning at Dollbright.

Dollbright fastened his gaze on the window hasp. His habit of concentrating his vision gave him a curiously formidable presence, as of one whose stern wits were gathered in an unfolded concourse. Most men are like leaking sacks; all very well if they lean on the hole, but unequal to the test of a prod. Dollbright still seemed sound and taut—if he, too, were weakened, no wrinkle betrayed the loss. The two regarded his obstinate and upright figure, then wagged their heads towards each other.

'Now then, what can you do? Typing, short-hand, book-keeping, of course. That's the least we want?'

Dollbright asked what more.

'We want a gentleman of good appearance, wearing good black, about your height, to answer the 'phone— '

They both exploded.

'What can I do? Crack your damned heads,' said Dollbright.

'Oh, you mustn't talk like that. We're all quiet 'ere,' said the man at the desk, while the other ducked his face behind a ledger.

'You're wasting my time,' Dollbright exclaimed. 'Are you in charge here, or are you a couple of spiteful servants playing rubbishy tricks while your master is away?'

They stared at him, taken aback. 'Give me an answer.'

'Since *I* am the master, as you call it, you've put your foot in it,' said the man at the desk, rubbing his withered little forehead as he took out a cigarette: 'Match, Jones?'

Jones lit the cigarette.

'He's a devilish hard man to work for—a regular smarting slave-driver, the tough old wretch,' he observed to Dollbright, beneath his hand. 'It's "my lord" here, and "your highness" there, and no end to the slogging. Look how it's wore me down! Why, I tell you it 'ud be easier for you to cut up all that wood with a hand-saw than satisfy him, and if you'll take a word of advice from a friend you'll keep clear of the fault-finding fellow.'

Dollbright's gaze swooped. The two fools felt it cut. Their fooling suddenly felt heavy on them. The one with the ugly nose wiped it for something to do.

'No, look 'ere, the job really *is* taken. My brother came in only yesterday.'

He had meant to be serious, but he could not help calling the other his brother, although he was no relation; at this they both roared again.

Dollbright turned in the doorway as he went out, and looked at the couple laughing like mean puppets in a lighted show— laughing to what but emptiness and passing time?

A toneless darkness had fallen on the roofs. The street was an illuminated groove. In the woodyard the bulky piles were blacker; the engine straddled its shadow in the corner as if it were hatching more of the reptile shapes around him, which with strained necks, like enormous tortoises, reared their wooden attitudes from the closer logs, and showed their cracked grey bark in the light from the office window. That broken square revealed a little night within the high walls. A night for all the town was hanging in the scaffold of the chimneys. The blind dog was still standing near the entrance, holding its head between its forelegs. A man and a woman had stopped to look at it, and Dollbright heard the woman exclaim: 'Why, he s blind! Poor thing, he's blind—'

'Ah, 'e's losing a lot now,' the man replied, and he touched the dog's head. The air was cold and wet, and smelled of mud: brown leaves had been trodden into the path. Long yellow lines ran down the gutters from the street lamps. A kind of short-lived, flaring stir agitated the town before the shops closed. Dollbright could return home by the Rats' Ramble, or take the road which led past Bridges's shop. He chose the latter; he wanted to see the place which he had left. When he arrived at it he felt a pang of pure astonishment that he should be no longer free to walk in and out of the door; that it was now, as far as he was concerned, most emphatically private property.

Leaning against the wall, end on, were several zinc pig-troughs, and Williams himself, his hands in his pockets, stood staring angrily at the road.

Dollbright stopped to ask him how he was getting on.

'It's too much for me; those bits of papers are in the bloody heart of a mess already. I haven't any head for that work at all. Well, I don't suppose nobody'll be dying to buy pig-troughs to-night, so they might as well come in. Lend us a hand, Dollbright.'

The old man spoke drearily, and looked very depressed. John Bridges' arrangements for immediate assistance had fallen through. Old Williams hated being there alone; yet the idea of a new face was loathsome to him. Drawing the hairy backs of his hands across his chin he complained in the dusky street:

'Why did you want to go off in a huff? Now everything's different. Heaven knows what sort of a hand the boss'll get in your place. Some slick fellow that scratches 'is 'ead with a typewriter, I s'pose.'

'Oh, what's the sense of jawing and grumbling—?' interrupted Dollbright.

'An' what's the sense of getting yourself into difficulty? What *are* you going to do these days? Still that's your look-out … this is mine. Curse it, look at the muddle! And I'd rather have that than one of them blame young fools piddling round the place.'

They brought in the pig-troughs. Williams switched on the lights. He did not mumble once, but talked on in a strong hoarse voice. Somehow Dollbright thought of a spider disturbed in its dusty darkness, and crawling forth into the noon, all grey and clotted with dirt and grime.

'Look at that telephone,' Williams lamented, 'been at me all day. I can't hear. What's the good of an old man of sixty-two, that was born before such things—'is ears aren't right. Well, out I'll go next, into the street an' be hanging on to my baby for my bread an' cheese.'

'Oh let it alone! it's done,' said Dollbright.

Mechanically he began sorting things on the desk, casting his eye on a pool of spilt ink that was dripping on to the stool. He felt uncomfortable. He was aware of blame, of scorn. His action was not virtue made clear: it was virtue hidden, which bit because it was not discovered. A man's honesty of conviction has a poor comforter in his lone self, when all's said.

Suddenly the telephone rang.

'You answer,' Williams whispered, jerking his arms and frowning.

'No,' said Dollbright.

Williams grabbed the receiver.

'Can't hear you … can't hear you,' he shouted several times, and over his shoulder to Dollbright, 'sounds like someone spitting down the line.'

'Here, give it me. Hullo … yes sir … yes it is. I'm—sorry. I looked in for a moment.'

He shoved the receiver at Williams.

'Mr. Bridges,' said he, and went down the street swearing madly.

Florence was sitting on the edge of a wooden chair, in the dining-room. She was dressed in her grey outdoor coat, but it was open, so that the ends were spread on the carpet near her feet. When Dollbright entered she was looking upwards at the scarlet geranium flowers which she saw through the wires of the bird-cage. Her yellow, waxy face shocked her husband. Yes, she said, she was ill; anybody would see that. But she added nothing to it, only put her hand over her eyes; his own were fascinated by the large buttons on her cuff.

When he found she would not answer him he stooped and coaxed the shoes from off her feet. She turned round on him then, drawing in her breath until her throat was a mass of agonized veins and sinews. That was about all he was fit for these days, she screamed. And mother had said he'd never see her want while he was alive.

'Your mother is dead, and her words.'

Florence glared, and rocked, and twisted herself around her venomous secret. Dollbright flung his hat and coat upon the peg and banged the street door because the rain was wetting the passage. He noticed Benjamin's large muddy footmarks going all the way along to the base of the stairs, and his cap, bulging from the shape of his head, which hung like a mouldy puff ball beside his own black hat. He loathed sharing his roof with Benjamin.

They avoided speaking to each other. Wandby's cheek was marked by a pale bluish bruise above his beard. He kept putting his hand on it and nursing it, but all the time his eyes were preoccupied by some remote thought. The house was dismal; draughts blew under the doors, the lamp seemed to burn palely. All the tilted faces wore sad, exhausted looks, like failing actors in poor lodgings. They went early to bed, while the town was still black and yellow, and the market clock mooned into the wet square below. The street lamp outside snapped out at eleven. Dollbright had extinguished the candle. Sight was gone, and then came sleep and dreams. He woke as the morning was getting light. It had stopped raining. Dawn wheeled over the opposite roof. He studied his wife. Her features were beginning to stand out from the blur of pillow and sheet.

Her nostrils were dark, her front teeth were long, her open mouth had grown old. Still it was hers. She breathed loudly. He thought this: the river that flowed beside me thirty years ago is the same river, in the same channel, though the waters are always new, flooding or falling.

Her hands lay outside the clothes. He moved, lifted himself. He became aware of a lovely sound in the sky. The wild swans were flying over the town.

In all the complaint of motion there is no more moving and unearthly music than this even cleaving of high air.

Dollbright's spirit faltered, then leapt upwards, to follow the riven wake of wings.

And close to his side another heart was feeding the frightful crab and rocking the destroyer. Infinite neighbourhood, provocative of thought from which nothing emerges; is there any answer?

Not in mystery. Not in perfect reason. Not in faith. After all, the most lucid revelation of God in us—is doubt. This is an odd way to tell a story—a bad way. It splutters like a lamp with water in the oil. Yet … Not long ago I saw a man with a twisted leg, who moved along in half circles. He must have seen more than most people; if one smiled behind his back, it was likely that the cripple's eyes would catch the smile. And supposing a man were set for an hour or two upon a slowly revolving wheel, he would come away from that circular path advanced in perception, if not in passage.

However, it *is* time to go forward.

It is so hard being dependent on silence when the whole town is seething with voices, lights and traffic. Feet are not only walking, but rapping, stamping and grinding into the pavement. In the cadaverous glare of electricity the people go swinging by. It is Saturday night.

I shut the window and go to the table. Downstairs a door slams repeatedly, and the floor shakes each time. There's an endless drip of disconnected conversation and harsh laughter, which frets me like a fever. I feel a useless energy. I am thirsty and confused.

IV

MRS MORRISS went into her husband's bedroom. He was lying on the bed twisting the broken binding of a book around his thick forefinger. His feet were crossed.

'*Are* you going out tonight? she enquired.

'I haven't made up my mind …' Ifor Morriss replied. He said nothing more. Mrs. Morriss glanced at him uncertainly and yet indifferently. The bed was a muddle, the room gloomy with dust and a dirty window. Mrs. Morriss was holding up the hem of her tussore dress: she moved her spectacles closer to her peering eyes, then turned round and went out.

He was glad when the door had shut on her greasy hair and sallow face. She was depressing, like this large dank Rectory, all stone and damp and obscurity. She sidled through doors and slunk along walls. She was stuffy and sly, and she liked to sit in airless corners with her feet on a footstool and the dog on her lap. Time was when Ifor Morriss had missed the sun and the light in the house, but now he too wished to rest, laze and dream in the shadow. His long meditations occupied hours. Many calls he did not heed. He did not want to break away from himself. But he thought of Dollbright and his own father's fierce religion. He remembered how his father had put him out of the back door; he had stood up against the mouldy plaster wall and heard the voice inside:

'For thy mouth uttereth thine iniquity, and thou choosest the tongue of the crafty.'

He remembered the backyard with its broken bricks, rank grasses and nettles, the chipped window-sill bearing a rusty cullender, and the flat sea beyond the neighbours' chimneys.

Had Dollbright sons?

Dusk wrapped his head, his arm, his long body, and rose towards the ceiling. An ashen twilight, grey and old, dwelt on the floor under the window. Bits of fluff stirred on the bare boards, and soft, curled feathers from a burst pillow drifted over fallen papers. Heavy tears of shadow hung on his eyelids. He drew up his knees, his hand clenched beside him. He might have been a dying man. He did not go out that evening, nor the next. But at sunset the following evening he went to find John Bridges.

The West burned and shrivelled. The hard hills swayed over the fields, led through the light like goats upon a string. Bridges was standing in front of the house, smoking. His red jaws could be seen from the back, a veil of smoke floated over his shoulder.

He took Ifor Morriss into a room with long lace curtains hanging from wooden rings.

'Cold?'

Ifor Morriss slapped his chest. His hands hung purple by his sides.

'Feeling queer and supine,' he sighed.

Bridges seized a brandy bottle and poured out a whole glassful of the stuff. Ifor Morriss drank it neat in two gulps. Nor was he affected in any way except to feel the better for it. His chest tingled.

'John, do you employ a man called Dollbright?'

Bridges stared:

'I did.'

'You don't now?'

'No, I've sacked him.'

He paused, and decided to leave it at that. Ifor Morriss looked at the pattern of roses and birds on the curtain. They stood out, white and thready, against the panes.

'I'm interested in Dollbright,' he said, 'the fellow has a vivid tongue. He burst in on me one Sunday night after hearing me preach, and spat holy damnation at me across the table.'

'And what did you do?'

'I listened.'

'By God!' Bridges exclaimed contemptuously. Ifor Morriss sat splodged in his chair, heavy, fleshy, enigmatic, rubbing his rough chin. His eyes gleamed with sly perception:

'But it was lovely! Think of a prophet in a black hat! Imagine a dogged seer in a hot mackintosh! He was a servant of Jehovah come to rebuke me with a stern and bitter rebuke. He has brows that bend upon one like a cloud, and eyes like waterspouts.'

He broke off. Bridges interjected:

'I see Dollbright on Saturdays in the shop. He is a clerk, not a bogey-man. I suspect his soul is behind his ear, and it's a fountain-pen.'

'I think it's a passionate and angry soul, and God have mercy on its passage—'

'Now you're serious.'

'So I am!' exclaimed Ifor Morriss, astonished. 'That's the second time he's got me.'

'I'm not interested in my enemies.'

'Enemy … enemy!' Ifor Morriss cried, becoming excited, 'that's it, that's he. A wild enemy to us and to our century, with the primitive strength to *condemn*. A bigot, but how one can fear him!'

'Only degenerates admire primitives,' replied Bridges shortly, and he felt his fleshy neck where anger seemed to stick.

'Ever so true,' Ifor Morriss mockingly conceded. He always felt he ploughed very stale ground when he talked to Bridges, just as Bridges felt irritable and childish with Ifor Morriss. He wasn't going to tell him why Dollbright had left. And yet he was very fond of the scandalous parson who knew him and his mistress in the face of the whole uncharitable parish.

Ifor Morriss stayed the whole evening. They moved out of Bridges' library into the drawing room, where the air was warm and smelled faintly of the Chinese silks upon the walls. It was the only room of its kind that Ifor Morriss ever entered, and he never saw the metal ceiling without thinking of the torn white paper, all wrinkled and cracked, that was pasted on the Rectory beams. Yet he thought that dust and cobwebs and ancient embroidery smelled much the same…

Barbara Cater sat on the coalbox. She had a high forehead with shining temples which she held in her hands. Those hands were exceptionally small, plump, and waxy white.

'Don't start an abstract discussion,' begged Bridges. She laughed carelessly. She was reading an obscure and incoherent book on the Compositions of the Arts which had been written by a friend. She showed a paragraph to Ifor Morriss, who had drunk more brandy.

'Any story can be illustrated literally or symbolically: thus, a man is presented in a field, hoeing. In occupation, setting, feature, he is exactly as the author has described him. The picture is an illustration of a particular man and a particular action. Another artist will present the subject symbolically, and it will not be *the* man hoeing, but *a* man hoeing. The first illustrates one story, the second all stories.'

Ifor Morriss smiled rather vacantly, not being interested, and gazed at the top of the fireplace. He reflected that it didn't matter if John *had* a crumb on his cheek, they were all such good friends.

'I don't see how a man hoeing can represent all stories, no matter how symbolically he's drawn. A man with a hoe is one thing, and a man up a tree another. They're both men, but a hoe's a hoe and a tree a tree. It's only their occupations that individualize human beings,' said Bridges.

'I think it's their clothes,' said Barbara Cater.

Bridges was filling his pipe: 'Oh, no, it isn t. A naked man asleep and a naked man driving a car are quite different.'

'Only for the time. All their habits and ways are the same.'

'You must tell me more about Francis Dollbright,' said Ifor Morriss suddenly. Barbara Cater sank her forehead over her book.

'Why?' Bridges demanded, and he felt as if he were peering down a well. Then he added, not briskly but decidedly, as he always thought and spoke:

'If you really do want to know something about him, I'll have to ask the old man. He employed Dollbright before he turned the business over to me.'

'I wish you would.'

'Right, I'll get a regular biography for you. But for any sake don't talk to me about him, for there's something in him that I don't like, that I don't want to remember—'

Ifor Morriss thought:

'That you fear.'

Days later he was sitting with his shiny knees pushed under the study table, scratching at a round spot of dried candlegrease with his nail, while he read part of a long letter.

'All that I know of Francis Dollbright before I employed him, is vague and unsettled. Probably I have forgotten much for my memory is bad now. I will tell you what I can. But remember that it may not be absolutely true, or rather, exact.

'His father was something to do with post office telephone work. He had to go abroad to Russia for nine years in connection with it, and he married a foreign girl from Moscow. Nobody seemed to be able to find out what was her nationality—some said French, some German. At any rate, she was not a Russian. Those were his parents. They lived in Manchester. If you want details I can give you them, as he told me things himself. He said that his mother was lame from falling downstairs, and that she had a very gentle nature. His father saved enough to buy the house, but Francis did not get a first-class education. He went to night school until he was nearly eighteen, and there he learned book-keeping. Of course, in my day a clerk needed to write a good hand— Dollbright's was a fine hand, but I'm not sticking to the point—'

Here Ifor Morriss clashed his teeth with impatience; glancing at a large oil painting of a white dog, he thought he would learn as much about Francis Dollbright by staring at its round dull eyes, as by reading this wandering letter.

'Curse the senile old fool,' he muttered, but after a moment he went on.

' … and I must say that it is very difficult to decide just what to tell.'

'I'd like more than any of this twaddle to find out what *was* his mother's nationality!' the reader interjected, 'that's fairly important if you want to trace a man's character; but instead it seems I've got to put up with his *education*—which never touched more than the outer life there.'

He grabbed the corner of the paper afresh.

'He took a sort of job as a sort of clerk under a bailiff on a big estate, but the bailiff had to go. At one time he was also clerk to a parish council in the Salus district. I fancy he was close on thirty when he married a girl from Chepsford, and at first they took in lodgers. He was always industrious. He told me he watched the Gazette for a job, and when I advertised for a clerk he applied and got it. He worked for me the two years before you took over.'

That was all excepting a note in John Bridges' hand: 'and thirteen years for me.'

Ifor Morriss was anything but even moderately satisfied. Among all this he had not been able to find a single explanation of Dollbright's vehement personality. He felt sure he would learn no more—the man was alone, unreadable, like a genius. There was no reason for him. His name, in the futile preamble he had just read, seemed like a powerful tide locked and degraded in the mouth of a narrow river.

He tore up the paper. He had come to the end of facts. The torn scraps fell on the table— fluttered in a draught. The door was half open, and through the aperture he saw the hollow of the hall along the passage and the spiral staircase winding close under the green wall. His wife was stepping down. She stooped forward, her heavy necklace dangled. He thought of her, he thought of Dollbright, and he thought of himself. In covering the three points of this vast triangle, the force of creation seemed far more immense than in spanning the planets… . He rushed outside. In the old yard, near a wooden door in the wall, was a heap of brush-wood. The door was hanging on its hinges, the blue paint was blistered. He seized a chopper and began to split chips to kindle the kitchen fire, heedless of the drops of water that fell off a dying tree on to his coat.

*

The same afternoon Florence Dollbright sat by a window clutching her knees in terror. She imagined her cancer as something alive in her body, something hungry and blind and revolting, like a worm. Hour by hour it was growing and ripening. She gathered her dress over the place in thick folds that hid her knuckles.

'I am dying. I must be dying.' She went out, unable to bear it in the room by herself.

With a rattle of nailed soles some boys burst from a brick alley.

'Journal, journal … !'

Their knees were naked, their faces raw and chapped. One wore a man's coat, another a pair of tin spectacles. They hugged bundles of *Chepsford Journals* in torn wrappers.

She heard the shrieks disperse. A man sitting loose-kneed on the edge of an open cellar kicked at a snail on the slimy step below him. The end of the street was red and far; the building looked false, like gimcracks at the back of a stage.

Florence tried to buy a bunch of violets, whose scent she loved. But all the men said there would be none until Saturday—there was no sale for them.

In the largest florist's she caught sight of a big green bowl full of them, standing to one side of the counter. The woman was just sprinkling the dark flowers with water. Florence pointed to them. The woman glanced contemptuously at the gnarled leather glove and replied that those were a special daily order from Mr. Bridges. Florence felt the cold air smart on her eyelids and lips as she walked along, Her face was yellow. A strand of hair which was too tightly pulled to the back, dragged at her scalp. She could not help noticing the smelly twilight which hung in the cracks of the town—in the open doors, in the arches of the Market House. She crushed a bit of wet purple paper under her foot. The gutters, running like sores, the black fissures in the pavement, the angles where the buildings met the ground all seemed filled with poison, with secret diseases ready to fall and feed upon the fair and tempting. Whole fruits plucked and piled to feed the sick; clean flowers to line and deck the mouldy grave; fabrics to wrap and wind the monstrous and revolting. The glare, the rattle and the paint of existence, which, with all its speed and dazzle or its drudging habit, was not loud or thick enough to cover the decay and terror. The rotten earth which was the foot and root of height, that was, at its most lofty, too low to lift from the worm's reach, *one* heart which knew its end!

All belief had gone. She had passed the Baptist Chapel with a thrill of scorn and a bitter grimace. Could the minister save her, or the prayers and hymns? No, only the knife in the hand of a man. Her orthodox hypocrisy was interrupted. She seemed to see the flow of people as a funeral procession, nodding at death. She stopped outside the chemist's. She stared hard at the bottles, the perfumes and the cut glass sprays in their frosty order. She saw one flagon with a ribbon—violet water, and immediately she went in and bought it.

When she had paid for it she made the assistant unseal it. She took a long breath of the scent. Next to her a short woman in a miserable khaki coat, was holding out a prescription. She looked absolutely browbeaten by poverty. After a moment she set her straw flask down on the floor and moved a step closer to Florence.

'Oh ma'am, excuse me, but you must let me thank you for the lovely eggs and butter!'

'Don't thank me, it was Mr. Wandby who sent them to you,' said Florence.

'Ah, but I know whose kind heart thought of it.'

Florence smiled. She was gratified, although the idea of sending Mrs. Johnson eggs for her rickety child had never entered her mind.

'How *is* Mavis?' she asked.

'Oh better, ma'am, thank you. I give her one for her breakfast every morning. Thank you again. I know how to be grateful. God evening, ma'am.'

Pushing the medicine in the straw flask with other parcels wrapped in newspaper she trudged away. She cleaned the chapel. Her husband was out of work, and her undergrown little girl could be seen any day playing in a narrow passage off Mill Street. Going home Florence did not give her a thought, but dwelt on the violets which Bridges bought for his black-haired mistress.

'Ah, if only my illness could be luxurious,' she said to herself, 'it might be almost bearable!'

If only Francis could afford to bring her bowls of violets, and pay for a white room to herself. If only pain had not to be borne in company, and groans echoed in other throats! She let herself into the house.

That night, after the Wandbys had gone to bed, she sat down again with her candle on her knee and said clearly to her husband:

'I have something in my breast.'

'What?'

'I have a growth in my breast. The doctor doesn't know what it is.'

He stood still, utterly horrified. His mouth was like a dark cord. The candle-light beat upon his forehead.

'I'm going to have an operation. That means I'll have to go into the hospital next Friday. He can't tell if it's malignant until … he's seen.'

He listened to her silently, then he sat down at the table and hid his face.

'Does it hurt?'

'No; only when I move my arm.'

As he lifted his eyes to watch her gesture, she saw the tears were pouring from them. They wetted a face which was stiff and changeless as an iron mould.

Later, struggling in prayer, he could only repeat:

'My God, my God, my God.'

*

It was seven o'clock in the evening, all the upper storey of Bridges' house was illuminated. The warm electrically heated air drifted along the passages and stirred the curtains in the archways.

Barbara Cater was still reading her friend's book. Some of it she understood. Some she thought she might come to understand, and some dazed her.

She leant on her waxen hands, her head was sunk, her shoulder blades stuck out sharply. A lock of hair touched her eyelids.

'It must not be forgotten in the struggle for expression that there are two main kinds of observation, the normal observation, which is spontaneous and perfect for reproduction, and the abnormal, which is deliberate and ruinous to an artist.

'For instance: you make a new acquaintance, and slowly or rapidly, according to your gift of natural perception, you come to know the shape of his hands. You are then ready to describe those hands, in few and just words without self-conscious detail. But if you have deliberately set a watch for the hands, said, as it were, 'I will make a point of "noticing them" you will come away with your artist's eye clogged with killing detail and, what is more, you will have missed the most vivid and necessary thing, *the main impression*, which, being the most important, strikes one first.'

Certainly that wasn't clear. The most important things don't strike one first, even if two people can be found to agree on what is the most important thing. But Barbara felt there was a logical conclusion behind the muddled words. She would try to rewrite the paragraph, to amuse herself.

She went to fetch a dictionary. In Bridges' own little room a man in a mackintosh with a black hat on his knee, was sitting with his back to the window. The room was warm, and the man's face was wan. It was thus that she saw Dollbright.

He rose, his wide open eyes fixed on hers. He saw the woman whom he remembered holding Bridges' arm in the town. Her hair was black, her cheek-bones high. She wore a plain dark dress, but there were several broad gold bracelets on her arms, and long gold earrings almost touched her shoulders.

He said that he had been told to wait here for Mr. Bridges. 'Yes. He will be in soon.'

She forgot to take the dictionary. When she was outside the door, she stood still.

'There's a devil behind and between his eyes. How some men hate me!'

She stepped out into the porch as if she were anxious for Bridges' arrival. She thought Dollbright an extraordinary man. She could see the outline of his head upon the curtain. It did not move, it might have been an omen. The porch threw a mass of shadow on the drive, beyond which lay the light from the landing window. In this pale oblong, footprints were visible. So few people came to the house that they could only be her own, her lover's, or this stranger's. She walked to them through the dark and stooped over them. They were not hers, they were too small for Bridges. They belonged to *him*.

The black forms of trees leapt stark-naked in the angular rays which pierced the night , in the direction of the main road. Sometimes there was silence. How fierce and white-cold were the stars, as if they were frozen for ever! it was freezing … winter was cracking the muddy ruts, breathing through the wired gate. The house loomed like a rock, holding the heavens in the angles of the roof. A deadly loneliness encompassed it.

The woman went in. She pushed a cushion under her head, and lay down on the floor. She spread out her arms; her breasts pointed to the ceiling.

Oh, beautiful limbs and vanquished breasts, is there nothing more to come?

From the dining-room she heard the sound of silver being

laid on the table. The door was open, and a maid was bending over the sideboard. The mistress lay like an idol in her stiff dress, with lacquered nails and pierced ears. The gold bracelets made it seem as though her wrists were thrust through rings and fastened to the ground. In the pattern of the carpet was a great green parakeet, flourishing its wings. The room was hot and full of crimson cyclamen. People on the road stared across the fields at the bright windows… .

Bridges came in late. He walked towards her in his heavy overcoat, his blue eyes wrinkled.

'Who's in there?'

'Somebody who wants to see you. He's been here a long time.'

'Know him?'

'I don't. He's rather remarkable-looking.'

'How?'

She could not tell him. But suddenly he guessed. He folded his arms.

'Now what the devil's he after? Wants to get back, I suppose. Out of the house he goes.'

He went towards the door. 'No one's indispensable to me.'

'I've heard you say that before.

Dollbright was standing in the centre of the floor like a post. The coffee that had been sent in to him was untouched. He looked straight at Bridges, and touched his forehead.

'How the devil you've got the face to show yourself here I don't know. It's like your damned religious impertinence. Get out.' Bridges shouted, his open coat revealing his large body.

'Please let me speak, sir' said Dollbright with an effort. By locking his teeth he repressed a violent fit of nervous shivering.

'Listen to you? No. You've got too long a tongue. But why am I wasting time on you?' Bridges cried. He opened the door wide and made a gesture of passing out. Barbara was standing at the foot of the stairs, listening. She seemed to Dollbright like a staring evil which he must face. He walked out of the door before he turned again towards Bridges and raised his voice.

'I've come to apologize and ask if you can take me on again.'

'Yes, that's easy: I've been expecting it. But no one's indispensable to me, you know.'

However, he sat down. One hand was flat on the table, his head was bent and his face in shadow. His ears were red from driving in the cold.

'It's all very fine to come here and apologize. You've got to explain yourself. I gave you time before. No one could say I wasn't fair. And your stool's taken. With so many really first-rate men out of work I picked up a good one immediately. For some time now I've been thinking the business needed a clerk who was a bit more up-to-date. There really wasn't enough doing at Mill End to keep a man on for that alone. I really want someone who can keep things straight in both shops. So it's no use going into the subject, Dollbright. If you hadn't *chosen* to go, I'd have kept you on as you worked for my father.'

'You can't overlook it and take me back, sir?'

'No; I'm afraid not.'

'Not even as an assistant? I know the business, even if I am old-fashioned. I'd do my best.'

'Well, you see we don't really need an assistant. And we've got to economize these days. So it would only be a favour, and you don't want that, do you?'

Dollbright stared despairingly at the figure of the woman leaning over the banisters.

'No man on earth wants it more. I never thought I'd have to beg a favour, and if I were strong I suppose I wouldn't,' he said with violence, ' if this lady near us—'

He broke off, bent his hand on the wall in a kind of blind need, and, like a man dizzy from a great strain, took an uncertain stride towards her.

'You have the power…you can—' She drew herself upright, close to the wall, and with both hands grasped her long skirts as if she would run up the stairs.

'What's the matter?' she asked distractedly, understanding nothing.

She peered with her short-sighted eyes at the two men below.

Dollbright flung out his arms: 'My wife's got cancer. She's got cancer!' he shouted.

'It's a lie to get you back without lowering yourself,' retorted Bridges.

'No, it's true. She didn't tell me … how could I know? It's true, it's true.'

Bridges walked up to him and stared at him.

'And how did you find out?'

'She told me, sir, when it was too late.'

He turned away. The crab had conquered. He had lost the pride of his severe laws. He had broken them. Oh, that he were outside, walking free. His breath laboured in his throat, his chest felt ponderous as if there were earth upon his heart. He thought: 'Your warmth burns me, and your flowers sting me. I wish I were alone. Oh my God, thou art not here!' Looking into Bridges' face he brought out his apology.

'I have been sorry for what I said, and I have wanted to tell you.'

'Is this necessity?'

'No, sir; it's fact that I had to struggle to keep myself from coming to you a week ago—'

The tumult of his conscience was visible as lightning in his face. It seemed that sleep would never quench his eyes; above them, his brows loomed like a coast. He might have been a man betraying a vile passion, ravenous and groaning wild regret, swearing to truth and begging of shame.

The pale intellectual woman shuddered with pity and revulsion. These were the footmarks coming to the house …

'Oh, John, for my sake, stop this awful scene. Take him on, or stamp on it at once.'

She raised her hands as if she would have clenched them in the air and shaken them.

'You're right,' Bridges scowled. 'Has he been appealing to your sympathies?'

'You know I never interfere.'

'Has he?' Bridges roared, and leaping up the lower stairs he pushed his powerful shoulder between her arm and breast. His great strained neck and craning head were poised like a toppling colossus; his mouth was a red crack in which she saw the strong blunt teeth, and the veins on his temples were swollen and throbbing. She seemed to see him as through a magnifying glass, huge, with horny nails, and a thick red skin stretched over his Adam's apple.

'No,' she said, 'no.'

'Do you understand why, Barbara? The damned crawler could ask for your help, he did, he dared in front of me, but he left because he thought himself too good to work for me.

Because he said he abominated my way of living. You're my way of living, Barbara, do you understand? He's famous for making speeches, but as far as I'm concerned he can hold 'em under his breath. If he had walked in here when I was out, and enlisted your pity, I'd have beaten his brazen head on that.'

He threw out his arm towards an iron gong near the door, and kept it there for several seconds, stiff with fury.

'He *didn't*' she cried.

'As well for him.'

'Won't you have me back?' Dollbright implored. 'I should have another view of things if I owed it to you. And what I said—it is undone… it surely is undone.'

Bridges gave a loud angry laugh. His hat was still on his head, tilted back. He snatched it off and threw it away.

'Oh yes.'

'He has apologized—' Barbara interposed.

The stiff figure of Dollbright in his mackintosh was planted square below them. The spiritual force behind his features was broken up like a star flying in fragments towards its tremendous encounter with a smaller earth.

John Bridges considered his clerk.

'All right. Apparently sinners have their uses. Thought you'd be a martyr, Dollbright, then found your wife was carrying the tail of your cross! Well, you can start again tomorrow, the same as ever and take charity with your wages.'

'At Mill End?'

He nodded.

'Thank you, sir.'

'Get out.'

He turned round and walked up the stairs, his coat swinging at the back with a swagger like scorn. A faint double-edged shadow dogged him—a poor weak thing for such a brawny man, that seemed worsted in an encounter with its kind.

Dollbright fumbled with the latch and his black hat. Outside he looked at the rim of the sky interrupted by the trees; at the side of the night the pines stood alone like ships returned to the quay.

Now no swans, or if there were, no following. That night John Bridges and his mistress had a conversation in bed. She began it.

'That man who came this evening reminds me of Ifor Morris.'

'Dollbright… how?'

'They're both mystics.'

'Mystics don't interest me. There's nothing in them. That's what mysticism is—nothing rolled round in a fog. As for Ifor Morriss, you've got your own notion of him and 'tisn't a bit like what he really is. He really is an old randy, given to drink and full of vices that are running to seed. Soon he'll be too old for anything, then he'll lie down and the spiders will spin webs in his mouth while he's asleep… You know, they say he robs the church plate, and the wine they use for their sacrament business is just old Llewellyn's port from "The Dog."'

He laughed out loud.

'I find him sinister,' she said.

'The devil would be a parson, if he came on earth I believe.'

They dozed, but the shrieks of a vixen out in the fields woke them. He laid his arm across her breast; the heat of his breath stroked her shoulder. It was very dark around the bed. She held his relaxed fist in her hand. They heard the cries again, dying in the petrified silence of a still winter night.

'John, are you afraid of death?'

'No, I'm not. Why should a man be afraid of going out? There's only one thing I fear.'

'What is it?'

'Pain.'

'Ah, I'm afraid of *everything*. I can't keep fear out of everything. It's like a dog lying with its nose on the ground—every movement I make its eyes follow, and when I try to get away from it it comes after me. You built this house to keep it out, but tonight it got in.'

'Do you mean you're afraid of people like Dollbright?'

'I suppose I do; I don't mind opinion as long as it's not cast in my teeth, but if it is I dread it. I dread the disturbance and the pointing. I'll face it, but I dread it,' she repeated.

He pressed her close to him, so that she could feel the spring of his body behind her.

'Darling, the man's only a helpless slave to some fantastic self-created taskmaster. His mind is barbaric and useless in a civilized time. What he thinks—if he can—goes for nothing. He isn't worth the food he has eaten. His god deserts him, which is to say he fails himself because he hasn't enough balance to steer his course. Then he runs to the atheist for help.'

'He was suffering tonight.'

'Oh yes, I know he was: it was a vile situation. Now if he had stuck to his decision right through his wife's illness and death, one might have honoured him.'

'It would be impossible … inhuman.'

'Yes. You might have had cause to fear him then. He'd be a formidable creature, if he could fill his outline. But he can't. He's a failure. Don't fear him.'

'Are you an atheist?' she asked doubtfully.

'You can call it that,' he answered. He paused, and resumed thoughtfully:

'It means nothing. Put your hands on me. You can feel all I am.'

She slid her hands over the swell of his chest and with each separate finger felt for his bones. He lay on his side like an idle implement in a furrow.

'A structure,' she said strangely, 'an arch enclosing space.'

'No, no, no. Nothing so enduring. Only a man grown from the womb enclosing a mortal brain. That is the source and the sum of all the mysteries, good and bad.

'While I live I am powerful, because I am complete. I don't need a faith, and I don't ask a god. And demons have no dominion in me. I *killed* the gods long ago,' he said, 'they died without a kick … a row of bogy men, smoky and dabbled in the fire of their makers' tongues. For how many ages have men slunk behind these monsters, and struck out under cover. I feel a frightful, a really blasphemous contempt for god-worship. Destroy it, and let's have a fair look at man. He is perfect in himself, or should be: if he isn't he's a faulty machine.

'What things I want this world produces. They are things that can be put in bales and sacks and travel by air, and road, and rail, and sea; they are things that walk in shoes and undress at night. And there are thousands of them.'

'Wonderful man didn't make everything.'

'Of course not; but that's no reason why he should go on leaning on blind creation, calling it God, and worshipping laws because he doesn't understand them. Man made man; man makes an end of man; he buries him, and forgets him. That's all there is to it.'

She had heard his voice further and further away, as if it were rolling down a hill side, and when he finished, a slight movement of her hand was her only answer.

*

In his mackintosh, with his shadowed jaw, Dollbright went on. His feet fell where they had fallen yesterday as he pursued his accurate tracks to the shop and back.

On the Monday that he started work again he told Florence where he was going. She sprang at him, and in a voice gruff with emotion cried out, 'My dear husband!'

Then his prolonged gaze seemed to hold her fixed. She slowly brought her hands together and clasped them in front of her.

'So we're all right,' he said. He smiled.

As he went out of the room she twisted round on her flat heel and stared after him, with her chin poking forward and her rigid hands against her breast...

The weather had turned wet again. Dollbright stood in the shelter of the back door, looking along the alley. The water butt was brimming; the surplus slopped over the rotten rim and spattered the stones. Mrs. Trouncer's clotheslines hung in slack loops.

Behind the high wall the Mill kept on pounding. The heavy shudders of the engine seemed as if they would bring down the whole worn-out house upon his head. Through the padlocked gate he saw the men with sacks over their shoulders loading the lorries, shouting and straddling unconcernedly on the doltish bags of grain.

Young Williams was there in the tallet dusting his hands

against his sides. His thick wet hair hung in writhing strands over his forehead.

The whole lot of them meant nothing to Dollbright. He fell into recollection. Once, when he was a boy of fifteen he had fought a friend until they had torn most of the clothes off each other, and had rolled about in a field with their skin flashing through the tatters.

Afterwards he had thought that his soul had died … no efforts would ever bring it back to life. He bolted the door of his bedroom and poured water over his head. Near the empty jug he knelt down, tied a scarf round his neck, and twisted it round his wrists. He meant to strangle himself; he was still young enough to think he could do it.

So fearful was his crying, that his parents had broken in with a hammer. He glared at them from swollen eyes.

His father pulled him to his feet and wiped his face. His mother kissed him.

'But what's the matter?' his father kept asking.

He could not explain that his soul was dead. But the terrible idea would not leave him until, impelled by lonely anguish, he confessed it.

'Mother, I've lost God. Shall I ever find Him again?'

She answered him calmly and wisely. 'Perhaps He will find you; leave Him alone to do His work. If we cannot draw near Him, He will come to us.'

'There's a black brew in me!' he burst out.

'And a very good one,' she said.

'Mother, do you believe the soul can die?'

'No, Frankie, the soul cannot die.'

He believed her then. But now he did not believe her. She was one like Ifor Morriss.

The soul could be destroyed, if it were unworthy. The man in the doorway and the boy with the scarf round his neck laboured in the same agony. So the memory returned and clung to him as the rain fell in the alley and made puddles in the broken stones.

Near the door an iron spout was dripping into a grated drain. Thick dusty cobwebs were stretched between it and the bulging wall. A scrubbing brush and knotted house flannels like grey fists had been put on top of an upturned bucket. A tabby cat stalked along the narrow ribbon of dry ground under the wall.

A sudden fury showed in his eyes. The corners glittered. He raised his shoulders and sighed under the weight of the hatred that he felt.

He hated Ifor Morriss. He hated Bridges. They had overrun him; he was down under them, and in this waste there was no God to set him up as high as them. He loathed them as the leaders of the armies of Saul and of David loathed the Philistines. They were anathema. He wanted to strip them, to burn their houses, to preach at them and see them beggars. God curse them!

He unfolded his arms and seized the door frame. His fingers ached under the nails, so hard he clenched them on the wood. He swung himself backwards, then forwards, his weight hanging on his grip. His feet were vices on the ground. The joints of wood below the cross beam cracked; a flake of plaster fell on him.

God curse them for the loss of him!

The cat shrank on its hind legs, its spiny back went up. Spitting, it bunched its paws and sprang for the top of the wall. Its ringed tail waved starkly. When his heart was quiet, he turned round and went in. He looked for Florence; she was lying on the sofa in the front room, pulling the fringe of the blind. She looked as if she were in a tragic mood. He sat down by her feet, cleared his throat and rubbed his knees. There was a pause. At last he sighed and relaxed.

'Florence, I've had rather a lot to go through lately; if it's made me queer I hope you'll forgive me. It's difficult being married, isn't it? I thought I was doing right.'

'You are a very good husband to me, Frank. My mother always said you would be.'

He said, 'I'll try,' and suddenly added; 'You are more to me at this minute than you ever were. It seems as if things have shaped themselves to show me how much our marriage means … it's my only way of peace. I want to stay in the house with you as much as possible. When you are well again, perhaps I'll go to chapel with you … no, no, that wouldn't be sense. Have you kept your faith?' he ended, lifting his eyes.

'Yes, I think so.'

She certainly felt no disinclination for chapel as she had the other night, but then she had not been thinking about it. Most of her friends had been to enquire after her, including the minister, who had sat with her for an hour and a half. A quiet smile settled on her yellow face. She told him Menna Trouncer was coming in to help while she was away.

'Oh, Florence, don't let us have any Trouncer here!' he cried in horror.

'I can't get anybody else.'

However, less than an hour later he had to confront Mrs. Trouncer, who announced herself by a rude bang on the back door.

What a face it was, and looking its worst! As the result of

a fall she had grazed it, and from ear to chin it was speckled with scabs which she had evidently been picking, then tried to cover the raw places with powder. One might have thought a cartwheel had rolled over the features, squashing and breaking and pounding them into their variolar disfigurements. The eyes slanted at him from their purple sockets.

Dollbright was griped with loathing. Was his wife's illness drawing this dank toad of a woman into his house?

'What do you want?' he demanded at a distance, as if he would restrain a too headlong charge against this most abhorred of his aversions, who had risen in his fresh tracks and flaunted herself in his doorway.

'When I want salt I put my hand in the salt cellar, and when I want a serious word with a man I go in and get it. Nor I don't come back again. I don't pick my teeth twice after one feed. So I'll step out of the rain.'

She did. He permitted her no more than a yard, which she fully occupied. Her great sullen mouth leant towards him; how vile was her squat neck, rimed with dirt, and her beldame eye!

Her voice, too, was a hoarse growl, as if the raw spirits had corroded the vocal chords.

'You'd say my daughter had a duty by me, eh?—and all the more by church and chapel?'

'Yes, and you to her, Mrs. Trouncer—all the more by flesh and blood.'

She sucked her cheek, and her eyes sidled from corner to corner. She was fierce and treacherous.

'Then you keep your eye clear that her and young Williams don't make sweet looks in your house—he's not up to her—or I won't let her come. And none of your church talk to me.

Flesh and blood it may be, but, Dollbright, there's more in both than you'll ever count. There's fire in blood and other things besides brotherly love in flesh, whatever the parsons say.'

She burst into a great clang of laughter, and rolled her thighs against the mangle, stroking her piston-like forearms. For all its brutality and malignity, a savage melancholia had hewn her face into something of a revelation.

Once more he noticed her short dirty neck disappearing in the wrinkles of a silk handkerchief. Suddenly he felt an abominable seduction dwelling in her swarthy flesh. She shook… . He looked at her with grim disgust.

'It isn't church and chapel and gory black hats that makes life,' she said.

'Nor whisky and the gutter,' he retorted.

'Talking of the gutter you name yourself. Sodding churchwarden!' she screamed glaring and advancing as he shut the inner door that Florence might not hear. When he turned round he found her face almost touching his ear; the large pores stood out like a rash, the nose was nearly black. Without the slightest warning but the audible clash of her teeth, she shot her fist out and struck him on the right arm above the elbow with her left.

He saw the blow whirling in the air like a chipped stone falling. She did not repeat it, she was too breathless.

'You … !' he shouted, 'touch me again and I'll call a constable.'

'If I'd the strength, I'd tear up the stones in the street to heave at you. I'd squash your bloody nob in the Mill, myself the wheel, and bless every fall of bad that comes your way. … I'd stamp you down in Hell, where I've been and seen not one devil but ten thousand holding up their arms at the whole—lot of us and sending up rockets that burst your eyes. Blast you to ruins! My tongue's gone down me gullet—'

She retreated, heaving all over like the sides of an earthquake. Her ragged hair slipped down the side of her face. Standing in the doorway she glared at him as if she would nail him to the wall.

'Church bug—climb up the cross!'

Then changing to a hideous mimicry of farewell, waving her hand and nodding with a truly vile smile:

'Good-bye, good-bye, friend! You hate everybody, but you can't forbid us to live!' and then she went. Suddenly, the door was clear of her. He heard her feet in the alley. All the heat in his blood seemed to have gone with her.

Passionlessly, with a slow torpid tread as though his legs were numbed, he crossed the floor, reached up to a shelf and took down a candlestick. He opened a cupboard, found a candle, fitted it in carefully and lit it. The light revealed him, pale and confounded as an accidental murderer, his face bleached, his hair slanting from the brows that he had tried to clear with his hands.

He held the candlestick aimlessly, moving it in a slow circle at the end of his arm. He sat down on a bench and put it beside him. The light now glittered in the corner of his eye, harassing him; it seemed to flow from his own brain, and streaming inwards, too, revealed the strong disruption there. He felt it, but he was too stunned to heed it at the moment. Only he turned his head away. Oh, why did his heart keep on beating, and, why didn't light go out before his eyes! He had fallen into the fire of his own condemnation, and it was insufferable pain.

He blew the candle out. The last daylight drained slowly from the whitewashed walls. Darkness was stretched on darkness. The Mill hands stopped work. His house was quiet, dead still except for a footfall in the front rooms, and a draught groaning in the copper chimney. Along Mill Street an accordion burst out jubilantly like a one-man revel, which ended in full blast.

His thoughts were changelings; they overran and teased him with their swift flight through his mind. He fell into a queer predestined mood. He saw the past as he had not made it; he saw influences moving the future which he could not avert. Whose were these malicious interferences in his life? What was the enemy of his highest efforts?

Ah, if it would manifest itself in a thing to be overcome or obeyed, it might be borne, but this agony of ignorance and dread was a goad beyond endurance. '*Something*, show what you are,' was his prayer, no longer to his open God, 'loosen the night or I shall die choking.'

He could not find words to form his thoughts, nor images to hold them. They wre too vague, immense, and inevitable. He had a sense of elemental diablerie quite apart from any human will. Men and things were part of it, as agents but no more. It was a dark illumination of the intellect, a search, a quest into the wizard powers. It was a faith prouder than any, savagely intolerant of happiness and goodness. It made Ifor Morriss smug, Bridges empty as the skull he preached.

It made Mrs. Trouncer great.

Instincts go deeper than reasons, sin than sanctity. Dollbright was, he bitterly and fearfully acknowledged, a swaddled ignoramus before this woman's violent force. She made him ashamed of his religion, weary of it and distrustful;

she interfused God and temptation. She was scored and branded. He hated her still, but he could think of her without the limitation of disgust. He ceased to curse himself for the abominable perversion of his desire. Self-blame was lost in an almost supernatural fear. He felt she was a giant figure in his destiny … she fated him.

What *was* she, less obviously than a blasphemous hag? She swilled spirits until her face was swinish and gloating, but what inexplicable look of initiation was that in her eye? Of what soul was her face the defiant scar? What end had she visioned and dared?

He knew that whatever these things were, they lay not *in* her, but beyond her; and that they had travelled to him through her.

She was a stupid, bloated and brutal drunkard. She would not understand him if he questioned her. She would scream at him and lift her fists. Or she would sit mute with drink in a deathly apathy, hanging her lip upon her breast.

He could solve nothing. He grew more and more wildly excited, twisting his fingers, knocking his knees, and screwing up his forehead against the spasms of actual pain. Under the reef of bone his eyes were lost and far from their calm courses. He was changed in the dark. All the time he was conscious of a new omnipotent idea of evil as a profound unearthly cause, a demonic oversoul, charged with life, and tangible only as breath. That was the nearest he could get… but the unsolid thought was pure with inspiration. He was not able to sustain it. His grasp was large, although he weakened now. Such moods lead up to madness or ebb from it. Dollbright felt mentally exhausted.

He noticed the open door was bumping against the wall

behind it, and his only desire was to put an end to it. He lit the candle again, shut and locked the door, and, after pausing in the middle of the floor, turned and walked through the kitchen into the passage. He took down his hat and coat and put them on in the street. He made his way to a quiet back road and paced the length of it several times. The lamps were few; here and there in some deep doorway or un-plumbed gutter lay an isolated scrawl of light. The monotonous action, the sound of his feet, and the cold drizzle revived and soothed him. He heard the brassy strokes of the market clock pick out eight above the roofs. He was tired out, and slowly he went home to sleep.

Outside Mrs. Trouncer's he stopped a moment. A lamp was burning on a bracket, and the shutter had not yet been fastened over the window. He saw the row of boots all with their tongues drawn forward, and the clothes hangers like bones, poking through the flimsy dresses. He lifted his hand as if to knock. But he knew there was no answer, so he passed by.

V

AS THE last days passed before she was to go into the hospital, Florence went to everybody she knew and told them she was going to have an operation. She grew very queer as it came closer. 'My husband is an angel. Nobody knows how good he is. I have never been so happy in all my life.'

Invariably she added her mother's prophecy that he would always look after her. How true were those words, she said! With wet eyes she beamed at everybody, clasping their hands as if she were about to die the next minute. She had never been gravely ill before, and she still felt no pain. The doctor had informed her that there was little danger.

He repeated this less strenuously to Dollbright; it was not the operation which was to be feared but what might be revealed by it. Did he wish her to be told the truth?.

Dollbright shook his head. No. Never. ' His attitude towards his wife was a contradiction of all his previous convictions. He felt hopelessly sad and bewildered. He did not pray. Through everything he watched his wife smiling in strange childish radiance.

'Oh, I have never been so happy in all my life!'

It was another evening, the last. The streets were close with yellow fog, the sky was invisible. Opposite, the shop bell was ringing continuously. The mistress of 'The Grapes' sent in liver pasties for supper. Emily came round with a bag of pears. Florence was eager to see her neighbours.

'They have the heart, Frank,' she cried. She was enraptured

when he brought her a cardboard box. In it was a silk dressing jacket, and a note from Barbara Cater, wishing her a quick recovery. But ought she to put it on, seeing who had sent it? It was so pretty! She spread it out on her knees, as she sat up in the armchair.

'Yes, wear it, of course,' said Dollbright.

Florence put it on at once. Her two small delighted eyes rolled around from face to face. The wisps of her grey hair twined on the silk, her appearance was strangely clumsy and bedizened.

'Well!' she ejaculated, and straightened her neck proudly.

Plumped on a footstool near the fire sat Mrs. Emily Jones, with her skirt inverted, absently putting her finger in a hole in her petticoat. Hers was the bland and charming expression of a good, lazy and peaceable woman.

'Menna went off to the pictures with young Bellamy Williams,' she observed, and from time to time opened her lap wide and looked at the firelight through the weave of her clothes.

'There's not many 'ud face an op. like our Florrie,' she suddenly declared, 'you've got real courage, my dear. Now if it was me, I'd be having a good cry.'

Indeed, tears were brimming over Florence's eyelids, but they only heightened the shining of an almost idiotic bliss. She lay back holding her husband's hand.

The Wandbys made their appearance in the doorway. Margaret came and sat down on the other side of the fire, but Benjamin would not enter. He stood holding his head on one side, the lamplight blurring the spectacles on the end of his nose.

'The house will be changed while you are away,' he said in a sad voice, which seemed muffled in his mouth.

'You won't notice the difference with Menna and Mrs. Jones to look after you!' Florence answered gaily. She sent him an eager smile; the poor thing wanted to be passionate friends with everybody. But his mind was already dwelling on Menna.

'Raining again, isn't it?' Emily Jones remarked as she drew aside to let Margaret share the fire.

The wind is south-west,' Margaret murmured, and she seemed to see the grey cowl twirling above the slates. She watched it for hours from her own window. Grey she was, sitting there with her hair in a plaited nob, stroking her black-mittened hands.

So the evening passed. In the pauses—and they were many—they could hear the barber's sign creaking on its rusty hinges.

*

And still it rained.

Somewhere like a stray tongue a bell was ringing. The slate roofs had turned a shining dark blue. A man in overalls hurried out of a wide open door into the Mill yard, and ran up the iron stairs. A pile of coal in a corner fairly sparkled, and the drops ran fast down the dirty bunged-up windows. Steam hissed, a hidden singer happily roared.

Daylight looked as if it had been spilt on the street. The cigarette-woman's children were quarrelling outside the shop window, with old coats flung over their heads. From the 'Bunch of Grapes' a raucous persistent voice proclaimed:

' 'Er was drunk as a wheel. 'Er fell over drunk as a wheel and bruised 'er face. Sudden. I saw 'er on the ground with a busted bottle, an' I said, "you ought ter be damned dead," I said, "you're no 'uman woman." " No I aren't," she says, rollin', "I'm one of God's wolves, an' I'll tear you into bleedin' strips." Awful to 'ear 'er talk, aren't it? There she was lyin' stupid right across the doorway, too 'eavy to lift. Drunk as a wheel—'

A taxi drove up to Dollbright's house and the driver knocked at the door, looking up the street as he did so. Dollbright and his wife stepped out, he carrying a suitcase. They were going to the hospital. Benjamin was in the passage, and Margaret, up in her window, was holding back the curtain. She moaned loudly to herself as she craned her head to look down into the street, without being aware of it, for her mind was dulled. Had it possessed the subdued vitality of her health, she had been destroyed by it years ago.

It was only a very few minutes before Florence and her husband arrived at the hospital. The white gates were open. Tin shelters stood on the lawn, and a tall poplar grew in a corner; the gravel drive gritted under the taxi. Raindrops fell into a yellow puddle near the step. A hard line of distant villas was ruled beyond the hedge. Florence seized his hand:

'Oh, Frank, Frank, come in with me!'

'I wouldn't go yet, if they tried to force me.' He rang. The door was opened by a young servant, who gaped at them as if to absorb their appearance through her mouth. They stepped into a red-tiled corridor which smelled clean, damp and disheartening. Florence's stomach sank. She broke into a sweat.

When she was alone with Dollbright, she collapsed on a chair, clutching his arm to her livid cheek, her eyes bolting. On one side of her was a ponderous marble mantelpiece, which seemed to engulf the room, on the other, Dollbright standing between her and the large window, stooping over her, so that she could see the same insistent strip of villas over the top of his head. At an equal distance the whole of Mill End, with its chimney, would have fitted into one pane; and of all its rolling din, its wheels, its nether engines, its reverberate bridge and stress of steam, not one remembered murmur in her ears comforted the trained quietness.

Gone was her unearthly joy. She felt her clothes wet on her back. She suffered horrible qualms, and cried into her hand:

'Oh let me go, let me go! I'm so afraid. Tell them you're going to take me home. I'd rather die slowly … do, do help me … do, do take me away. Frank, Frank, oh, Frank.'

Tears hung at the corners of her mouth. He tried to cheer her, but the words mocked him. They sounded broken and hapless.

'You won't feel anything. You'll soon be well—'

'I want to ask you something, Frank.'

'What is it, dear?'

'You do think something of me?'

'More than anything in the world.'

It seemed as if he were delivering her up.

'I shall be lucky and come through all right. I've never been ill in my life, and that'll help me, won't it?'

'Of course it will. You're a strong woman. Don't you be afraid.'

He had never wished to be rich before, but now he would have liked above all to be able to give her everything she wanted. Their ordinary selves were gone. In their eyes, which were locked upon each other, shone the helpless dazzled light of passion, but it was the passion of fear and imminent parting, the extremity of time when living is held up by a terrifying obstacle, and there is no glimpse of the course beyond it. Then the matron entered. It was only a cottage hospital, and she was not too important to retain friendly manners. She called Florence 'My dear,' and while her prominent eyes took in the details of the stained and weary face her brain said briefly: 'hysterical.'

She did not like the look of Dollbright, but felt certain that his wife would be easy to manage.

'Now,' she remarked, scanning them, and holding herself very upright in her white dress, 'Mr. Dollbright can go with you as far as the ward if he likes, and then he can bring away your clothes.'

'Yes, I will,' he said.

He walked a little behind Florence up two shallow flights of stairs.

'Here,' said the probationer who had led them.

Florence gave him both her hands.

'Don't cry any more,' he whispered.

'No; and don't worry about me.'

'Good-bye.'

Florence went inside.

There were three other women in the ward who turned their heads towards her, and one who did not move. The nurse said she would bring a screen, and Florence undressed behind it. It gave the illusion of a wall, but not of privacy; the women's talk was too clear. A laugh sounded.

'I say I shan't let my husband come to see me here again, or I shall lose him. He spends all the time by *your* bed.' Three laughs.

Florence wound her dressing gown tightly around her and

arranged her clothes in the suitcase. She moved towards the door. The nurse quickly stopped her.

'Where are you going, Mrs. Dollbright?' She asked abruptly, and she took the case from her with impersonal authority.

'I was going to give my case to my husband. He's waiting outside in the passage. Please let me have it… I want to give it him myself,' Florence explained agitatedly. She put out her long thin arm, tears were glimmering between her eyelids.

'No, you mustn't tire yourself. Your husband's waiting downstairs. I told him to. I'll take it. It'll be quite all right. Now you get into bed.'

Florence slunk behind the screen. A hopeless sob broke from her, like an interruption in the women's conversation. She stared upwards; the lofty ceiling seemed crumpled by her tears, and a pale, pale foreshadow of evening was floating imperceptibly across it from the inner wall. She felt Frank's departure as painfully as if she were forced to watch it, to watch him go home.

When she was lying in the cold bed the screen was taken away, and she was able to see the formal arrangement of the small ward.

Like a hot water bottle?' asked the nurse, fresh in her blue dress.

'Your feet are stone cold,' she said, as she put it in, and she pinched Florence's toes as if she were an infant.

The strain eased.

'Nurse, is it going to hurt very badly?'

'Bless you, no! You won't know anything about it,' said the nurse, heartily.

Florence laid back her head. She wiped her face, and

suddenly, with a profound sigh of weariness she relaxed. She had only to be still. Living and dying were not her works.

The fire was red behind a wire guard, the floor shone, the nurse's uniform rustled. Everything was enamelled, polished or varnished. The unswept world of the whole was gone.

Outside it was as if a great palm had stroked the poplar…

They operated the next afternoon. The sun was shining above oily yellow clouds. The streets and roofs were unhealthily glazed, and as Dollbright rushed through the crowds, his mind was filled with the followed image of death pacing these ways.

He glanced dreadfully at the operating theatre. The probationer, who met him at the entrance of the hospital, started uncontrollably, and her aghast hands moved at random towards her own heart. She forgot to show him in and they remained standing in the doorway.

'Yes … I … yes, it's over. The doctor's just come out—'

Suddenly the matron was there, without her head-dress, her white hair loosened like a storm. Her apron was actually marked all over the front with the blotches of his wife's blood, from fresh pink to deathly scarlet. Though controlled, she spoke on the brink of distraction … her feet might run, her open mouth might be the vent of calamity.

'If you run you might catch the doctor. I saw him going towards the gate. He can tell you.'

She turned round to hide the infernal life-lasting map on her.

Dollbright ran. The doctor was just about to drive away. When he saw the man fleeing to him he turned himself sideways to talk.

'It took longer than I expected, it was very large and I had to remove the whole breast. She's not in any danger.'

'Was it malignant?'

'Yes. There's no need for any examination. I knew as soon as I saw.'

Malignant. The word struck downwards into the masses of his silence. He linked none to it. The doctor raised his head to look at him enquiringly, and found that he was already yards away. Buildings and pavements slid under him … in his dazed eyes the mottled sunlight changed to an unblotted red. He walked, unaware how fast. The pattern rose, defined in the flaked water of the wind-rasped river, in the olive shadows of the withy branches. The congealed sun stood over the centre current. Was this dull drop the same broad lobe of summer spreading oil on scars? To-night there would be no light on the grass, but the stars would string shadows on the roofs…

He realized where he was. At the far end of the landing stage a young man in a faded cap and a khaki shirt was doing something to the bottom planks of a boat, upturned on trestles. Damp oozed in the cracks between the tarred planks. The cold tawny water slapped the piles, and the young man's hands looked sore and swollen. His braces were cutting his back, his coat lay across the end of the boat. The sun was in his eyes, too, but he saw it ordinarily like the bottom of a glass, round, small, shining through a tear in the clouds.

Dollbright sat on the landing stage until the worker gathered up his tools and, swinging his coat on his shoulders, took himself off. Then in the same sullen agony as when he came, Dollbright went home. Margaret Wandby saw him go upstairs. He stayed there until supper, except once when he went out to telephone.

At supper he sat with his arms on the table and his clenched fist denting his cheek. One side of his face was grimy. It was dust. He had been lying on the attic floor.

The brother and sister were free to look strangely from his frown to each other. He intercepted no glances, and seemed to heed no words. When he was asked to carve, he passed the knife and fork to Benjamin, saying heavily:

'Excuse me, but it's of no use to watch you. I can't eat, and so I'll go.'

He stood up. His eyes were fierce and keen as if he were close to an enemy.

'The fact is I am upset and I might offend you by something I say or do; it is horrible to see food on the table … good night!'

Margaret bent her head meekly.

'Before you go, do let us know how Mrs. Dollbright is?'

'She's very ill,' he replied in a rough voice. He passed blindly out of the room, and they heard him on the stairs. He seemed to pause on the landing, then the thudding uncarpeted footsteps ascended to the top of the house. They did not like the sound; it was queer and rousing. Soon they heard another.

'He's fallen!' Benjamin cried, rushing to the door, 'Hi—are you all right?' There was no answer.

'This is an unfortunate house,' Margaret muttered in the uneasy silence.

Benjamin grabbed a candle and ran. At the foot of the attic stairs he held it up and was able to make out the shape of Dollbright sitting ghostily beyond the scoop of light.

'Oh, Lord, are you hurt?' he panted.

'No,' said Dollbright, very roundly.

'What are you doing?'

'Sitting in the dark.'

'Oh.'

Benjamin hesitated, wiped his hand on his hair, and, turning slowly, descended once more. His shoulders and the top of his head sank out of sight. Dollbright hid his eyes. His hand was his only shelter. He had fallen after striking a match, and in a moment of pure frenzied exasperation he squeezed his temples between both palms, and rubbed them so violently that his head rocked and the floor under him seemed to sway deliriously. The darkness was full of derision. He ground, he ground within himself... .

The mice crackled under the rafters, nibbling at his worn control. 'Be quiet, be quiet,' he whispered, and then shouted and then stamped. He scraped his lips with his nails, his trembling fingers crept lightly as shadows over his neck. How did a man tame his angry heart? How did he bear with his burning, wretched, miserable self? How did he live?

'You *shall* rest—flesh promises you that.'

He knew that at last, and far away he wanted to die. The weevil was through the skin. Every thought ended in the shock of his wife's cancer. He did not know if he loved her or if he felt deeply repentant towards her; only that he was separate from her and from everything but his clinging self and the terrible reality of self. Pain was his own, and sin was his own, and grief and trouble. In others, try as he might to measure them, they were only reflections of what he had to endure— or end. Consciousness settles unshakably on a wound. Florence had cancer —he stared at the horrible fact, groaned over it, tried to plan for her remaining happiness, but over and over again the itching of his soul recalled him to himself, himself, himself, sore, worn, collapsing.

The street lamp went out and he was no longer able to see

the warped line of the window sill. He saw instead the landing stage and a figure like his own run across the leaping planks and plunge headlong into the numbing water. Dollbright put his hand up to his mouth. Leave Florence like that now, to live a few months or years uncomforted? Vile ego… .

He heard the rain swishing, gobbling and churning in the spouts and gutterings. Oh for dead, blind sleep, years, seasons of it, to suck and not restore the strength to rear pangs and rages! Could he sleep? Let him, and not dream tonight. He was cold, cold. The night was built around him like a shaft. Whenever he stirred his arms and legs he touched anew its cold black surface. *Could* he sleep? Let him try…

He went to his room and threw himself in all his clothes on the bed. Out of a heavy doze the first cock crew, the sky emerged, the town was lifted up in the morning. The south wind blew shaking the blind; he sat up with an effort, rocking, as if his spine were all that was holding him together, and grasping his shoes by the heels, picked them off, and cast them on the floor like scraps for chance to blow away. He wrenched off his collar, and in turning his chin, felt the stiffness above his eyebrow, where he had knocked himself. He fell back, humping his shoulders.

But he could not sleep again, so he got up and looked at himself in the glass. How grimy, weary, sunken was his face! It was pale, not glaring, but damned by the eyes. God had punished Florence for him, God had sown the cancer in her breast, and it had thrived on his sin.

*

He went to work. At one o' clock old Williams rang the Dollbrights' door bell. He was in his drab overall, which was wet. One foot on the step he peered up and down the street with an unquiet scowl. Benjamin opened the door, his hand hovering about his beard.

'What?'

'Has Dollbright come home?'

'No,' said Benjamin, 'I don't think he has yet. In fact, I'm sure he hasn't.'

'Listen, hark, Mr. Wandby: somebody ought to keep an eye on him—he's strange, he's queer. The rain's got into his head I do believe, yesterday he didn't come to work at all. This morning he walks in with a blame great bruise on his dome. Didn't answer me when I put it to him why he hadn't shown up—wouldn't say anything about that purple thump. At eleven-forty-five by this—' he dived into his waistcoat pocket for his watch and dangled it from a foot of steel chain—'he went, hat and coat and all. I shouted, "where are you off to?" And he said "I *can't* stay at that desk."'

'That's what he's paid for, Mr. Wandby, whatever his trouble. The way he's behaving is no game to play when he's scarcely patched up the last lot of difficulty. I'm going back now … there's no sense in everybody losing grip with their toes, and if Mr. Bridges should hear of me locking up in the dinner hour, bang goes my job, and I'll be hanging up my stocking in the Union come Christmas. I wouldn't have done it if I didn't feel there was something up with my comrade in crime.'

'Thank you very much for coming. But wait a moment. If Dollbright doesn't return here or to the shop what would you suggest doing?'

Old Williams considered the toe of his boot. 'I don't know; I s'pose there's nothing we can do. He'll turn up to go to bed. But he's a fool,' he added fiercely, 'I meant to tell him. And his wife in hospital. Good day, Mr. Wandby.'

He turned his screwed back and scuffled away like a beetle making for a crack.

Benjamin drew the damp air deep into his lungs and sighed it out: 'This hopeless rain,' he said, shutting the door. He stood in the glowing passage, thinking. From the memory of his own severe trial sprang a sudden fear for Dollbright. He took a step towards the door, stopped, then slowly and wearily passed his hand over his forehead. The dusky bulk of his body bent forward until his head was pressed against the wall.

'I shall begin telling tales out of nightmares,' he mumbled indistinctly.

*

Benjamin's sudden intuitive anxiety was ahead of fate. It was visiting day at the hospital; at two o'clock Dollbright was admitted to see his wife for the first time since her operation the day before.

Her appearance was terrifyingly changed. She lay propped up on pillows, weeping out of enormous, distended, red-veined eyes. Her lips were crusted and swollen like rubber. The nurse warned him not to be disturbed by anything she might say, and not to stay long. She was still dazed by the anaesthetic.

'Here's your husband come to see you, dear.' Then she left them, as if she were lending them to each other, by special kindness. He leant over the bed, kissed Florence and touched her arm timidly. She went on crying with those monstrous, unrecognizable eyes fixed in her head, which rolled from side to side, so that the tears zigzagged over her cheeks and nose, leaving sore-looking tracks.

'Florrie dear,' he said close to her face, 'How do you feel?'

'Dreadfully ill,' she moaned in a low dazed whisper, 'I am dreadfully ill.'

She feebly prodded the bedclothes near her chest. All her life seemed to be in her fingers, in her tears and her uneasy head.

With a sickening effort she fixed the awful eyes on him…

'Pain here … such pain here—'

The nurse glanced across at him and flashed him a strong smile. She took a paper from the table drawer, held it in front of her, then put it down in a hurry. The draught of her stiff dress touched Dollbright as she swiftly passed the end of the bed.

The visitors' conversation waxed like a mob conspiracy; beneath the peculiar tones ran a sinister and suggestive whispering as if they were choosing a victim. There was a flickering of eyes from patient to patient, a disturbance of lockers, a faint smell of thick clothes and wet boots.

Dollbright pulled a chair close to the bed and sat down. He drew forth his handkerchief and softly dried his wife's tears. Suddenly he heard a voice shouting:

'Stumbling stone!'

Trembling with shock, he let the handkerchief fall on the sheet. He had uttered the guilt of his inmost heart.

But when the shout was repeated, he realized that it was silent, though it over-cried the roof. Tenderness withered under it. He sat smitten, his ears opening as the door of Hell. The secret whispering wound into his brain, which bolted it within. These people knew he was a hypocrite; they were discussing him under their breath, they would take his name home in their mouths... He looked stealthily and intently around the ward. In the furthest bed, under the rain-dimmed window, was a woman with a shiny white face, flat on her back, and waving her hands to emphasize her replies to a young man who was standing near the locker. He was holding an orange and gently feeling its texture against his cheek. A fat, oldish woman with sly moving eyes and a sagging lap was sitting at the patient's head. She was bursting with laughter; her nasal, dragging voice was clearly audible, though the words were indistinguishable.

The visitors to the woman next Florence, were three women, all large, with bulky shoulders; they kept changing place, stooping, raising themselves and turning their heads, so that he could only catch glimpses of the people attending at the two beds beyond them. He listened carefully. It seemed to him that these hidden ones were the whisperers, and that now and then a slithering flashing pair of eyes probed his, and a disdainful smile mocked him.

'I must watch them,' he said to himself. He picked up the chair and carried it round to the other side of the bed, so that he faced the whole ward as if it were a wide corridor. In great distress he watched the people going from one bed to another with ease and familiarity. If only they would not whisper he could defy them, ask them publicly which of them had not carried a dreadful word or name in their hearts. Had the pack not fastened on him, they would have pulled down another. He straightened his neck, opened his eyes wide and folded his arms; but all that was no more than a deliberate effort not to fall on his knees beside Florence and hide himself.

He fumbled in the pocket of his mackintosh and produced a white box of grapes.

'Look!' he exclaimed loudly, holding them up. He opened the box and rustled the tissue paper. Then he felt in the other pocket, and laid a bottle of eau-de-Cologne near Florence's hand.

The nurse entered. She stood inside the door observing Florence. Then with a bending sweep she passed Dollbright and contrived to mutter:

'I shouldn't stay any longer.'

He started and looked at his wife. She lay exhausted. Her eyes reminded him of great dim lights coming out of a tunnel. He noticed the stillness of her hair, which used to wave from the back of her neck in short feathery wisps.

'Frank—'

'I'll see you again soon, Florrie. Don't cry any more.'

'Is it… still raining?'

'Yes,' he said gently. _

'Oh… oh… oh, when will it end, when *will* it end?'

'Never mind, never mind.'

A dreadful expression of baffled fear contorted her face; she clung to his wrist, but moaned at the pain the movement caused; clearly she hardly knew him and cared nothing for him. He kissed her, muttered something, and escaped from the ward.

He felt that he had experienced true horror, and nothing could efface it. He was loaded with guilt. He could not forget the cry that broke from that taunting self which lay beyond reach. He could not suppress that. Oh God, release me from my demon or I cannot *cannot* endure to live. He could not think what to do with himself. Something inside him was threshing in every direction, like a sudden awful pain which must be ignored and concealed, or like a clinging dream which fights against the morning. Fear of vision, and fear of truth, fear of death and life and God.

He was in extremity.

He returned home not seeing the full streets. The expanding mind wears huge environments like a skin, and at times fills all boundaries without a seeing gap. Dollbright stopped at his door, inserted the key, and, after hanging his hat on the peg in the passage, went upstairs to the attic. It happened that Benjamin was descending, and the two men were obliged to pass in a very narrow space. In the midst of his turmoil Dollbright knocked against him roughly, but as unmaliciously as a wave jostles a boulder, nor did he pause.

But Benjamin did. Holding on to the banisters by both hands, he craned his head upwards, his beard twitching. He groaned, or swore, one could not distinguish which, and remained standing with a livid face and eyes staring upwards at the dark and heedless figure of Dollbright mounting the higher flight. Then with a strange mistrustful expression, afraid, secretive and defiant, he too moved, and vanished into the gloomy passage.

This peaked room again, these grained rafters, and trunks and wide window sill, with the circular stains of flower-pots, the distracted finger marks on the dusty floor! He plunged inside, locked the door, and leaning against it, closed his eyes in a state of giddy despair. After about five minutes he roused himself, and asked:

'What am I doing? This isn't what I came here for.'

Again he seemed transfixed. The eyes in his downbent face, though open, were immovable. They stared and stared until the growth of agony behind them made them glimmer passionately, and he screwed his wrist in the hard grasp of the other hand. The left against the right, and the loss of one makes the survivor cripple. 'Oh, God, keep me from praying! I will not pray,' he said.

He had forsaken God, and God had forsaken him; so let there be no more between them. He was no Naaman. Truly, fervently as ever he could acknowledge:

'Thou art God.'

Never again:

'Amen, I am thy servant.'

He was bemused by shock, as one remembering where his senses left him, and vaguely feeling rather than recalling their foggy march beside his spirit in the loomings of unconsciousness. He went back to the hospital ward: he heard again his vile thought screamed grossly in his mind; he saw the evil in himself like a humpback's swollen shadow, not only hideous, but indissolubly *his*, for ever his on earth, an unchanged stain, a midnight contrast to his aspirations, yet owing its existence to them. A man indeed, and not in the first millions, who was lost by the commandments.

He turned his thoughts. He must be reconciled to existence. He must struggle now, or risk a nervous illness, perhaps even madness and suicide. He saw his danger: he must make a bargain with his just demon.

'This life to me. The next, if my soul lives, to you.' He folded his arms to feel the strength of bone against him. His chest was shaken by a sweaty trembling; in the cold attic a strange heat clotted his veins. The thing, whatever it was, that he was here to quell (conscience or demon whose loud voice he feared to utter and betray himself) had reckless control of his pulses. If long wear results from steady usage, then Doll-bright threw away a year of life in this crisis of his contradictory elements, mystic and material. Looking at the walls he felt a frenzied impulse to smash himself against them, to stamp on the floor, to jump from the window. He understood the gnashing of teeth and the search for any antagonist to be the proxy of the inner enemies. He understood insanity. No wonder maniacs beat upon their foreheads in a vain attempt to reach the torturer, and failing there to gain relief, bore a grudge against the very air they gulped and gaped, being void!

But this was worse than the hospital! The more he gave way to these extreme feelings, the greater and closer grew the danger. He mastered his trembling. He would have to watch himself. How easily and powerfully his emotions now affected him! That alone showed him the progress of his weakness.

He moved and seemed to grasp himself at last.

He must and would forget the distortion of his soul, now and forever unchosen; he would exist on earth at least, like better men; he would lead a calm sane life, shielding and cherishing his wife; he would put away his faults by resolution; look outwards, walk on the surface, close his jaws on prayer. He would, he took his oath. The feebler he was now, the stronger he would be. He was joining life, which was to be heard drumming in the street below and in the choral distances, which was uplifted on its own voice and overwhelmed dissent. It drew him to the window, literally, for he found it terribly hard and exhausting to pull himself upright from the door against which he had been leaning all his weight…

Putting his two hands upon the sill he gazed down at the unappeased motion with hatred and resignation. It seemed to quake and coalesce, and gather knots and tangle. His stare plunged into it, till like a quicksand the grey mass of men and stone sucked him down, down, down. His senses rushed out of his eyes—he had a second's vivid thought that he had fallen from the window. But recovering, he found himself upon his knees clenching his fingers round the hasp which had impressed rusty prints deep in the flesh.

Below him traffic squirted mud and water at the pavements. Wheels sounded as if they were tearing a skin off the road, and blue reflections travelled swiftly under the bellies of cars.

Movement, wandering, restless, tragic, hard upon itself. If only, like a chain, it were being safely coiled away upon its rounds within a starry-lidded box, outside dimensions!

Is there a symbolic meaning in the yellow cock who treads the weather, that these days in shape instead of voice, he still recalls attention to the prevailing wind?

Reared on a warehouse, and higher than the scaly intervening roofs, there was one showing in the square of the attic window, and glinting like a spark in smoke. Dollbright turned his back upon it.

*

He seemed to have fallen asleep with his head hanging. Wakening in the dark, he saw a faint light shining through the large wooden keyhole. He dragged his limbs together. They were stiff on the surface, as if sweat had dried on them, but all the heat had shimmered out of him. He was so cold that his shivering body scarcely warmed the clothes which covered it. He longed to get to the fire. Someone had placed a lamp upon the topmost stair; the circular wick, turned very low, was blue and creeping, like a glow-worm, and its colour recalled an evil memory … of what? As he brushed past he saw Ifor Morriss again, as he had sat close under the lamp that evening in his chilly study. But it was a paralysed vision. He seemed unimportant, the mere remote cause whose effects had absorbed all the fatness of his deed. A withered root. Dollbright sighed, it was all that he had in him then.

Weariness, weariness, weariness. Each separate limb was in its own sleep. He was so tired that as he walked with open eyes he muttered, 'sleep … sleep—'

He kept his resolution. He altered, one said, even in his face; it was stern—that it had always been—harsh, and that was new. Yet for the peculiar quality of his expression, Benjamin, his closest watcher, could find no single word, nor can I; it is best arrived at through the contrast of what had been … no, nearer to a definition is the exposure of some deep strata which catastrophe had opened. Depths pushed upwards, the airing of foundations. Benjamin saw a small landslide on one of the hills above the town. A placid footpath was buried under tons of earth and red rock. A particular stillness seemed to have descended on the heap: it should have smoked or shown some transitionary stage to blend the change. The very grooves and raw scores of the fall intensified its awful immobility, as movement does intensify a subsequent stagnation. The same branch-threaded distribution of light shone on the difference, as on the surrounding ground. Why was the Mill closed so solemn an opposite to its working self that the very machinery was an effigy of utter discontinuation? Why is a dead man so preternaturally motionless? Because

alive, he *moved*, and yet his form, his contours, and his look
are at least a twin's likeness. That likeness is the difference—
the difference between air and vacuum. That was how
Benjamin saw Dollbright's face afterwards.

*

At half-past ten Benjamin let himself in with his own key.
There was no light in the passage; his feet and all his body up
to the neck were hidden, but through the glass square above
the door, the street lamp threw a long ray on the wall over
which the shadow of his head, with its sharp nose and prickly
beard, glided out of sight.

He shuffled to his room, trying to smother the sound of his
footsteps in the quiet house, and lit the candles in the tall
candlesticks. The room was foggy and dingy as an old man's
bedroom often is, almost as if a kind of brown stuffy mist has
settled around everything. A tie hung over the mirror, a pair
of shoes stuck out from under the bed.

Benjamin shut the window, which gave on the Mill yard,
and still in his overcoat sat down on the side of the bed. With
one foot he softly, rhythmically kicked the wall. A patch was
worn there by the monotonous action. Dully it thudded, dull,
dull, dully. Now here, now there, now on this wall, now on
that, for nearly twenty-seven years had appeared the mark of
his unquiet foot. And as it swung he argued aloud with himself
in broken tones.

His nights were infected by his past more deeply even than
his days, and his sleep ran always neck and neck with dreadful
dreams. The household was used to hearing him shout; often
there were noises which seemed as if he were shaking the end

of the brass bed, or tossing himself with furious impatience from side to side—this heavy, unimpassioned, old man! Calm, contemplative, as he seemed awake, there *were* loud brassy cries in his sleep, there *were* crooked echoes, upheavings and subsidings. He made his nights short as possible. He could not escape however. Tonight he undressed and lay reading until two o'clock. Even as he blew out the candle with a drowsy puff he knew what was to be released in his brain. He dropped straight into the anticipated nightmare.

As usual he was in a small room, bending over a table. He walked around it, still in the same stooping attitude, and fumbled with the handle of a drawer underneath. The action was intolerably slow; he saw everything as clearly as if he were awake, but somehow it took years to see. The drawer was locked. He paused for centuries, and then came the awful shock of being overlooked which often woke him. This time it did not, the dream continued. He looked up and there was Francis Dollbright behind him.

'What have you done?' the vision said.

Benjamin knew the answer was the final test of himself; he knew, too, that really he had made Dollbright his judge, and that through him lay peace, but he did not, could not, speak. He was afraid. It all faded. He thought he awoke, and seized the matches. And then a hand came forth from the bed and snatched them from him. The bed was crawling with hands, like reptiles. They were his! A shudder woke him.

A nerve in his back was pulsing as though vitality itself were for a moment arrested. It was only feeling … but what utter feeling! Every organ in him seemed to have stopped, and the little thread of existence had so dwindled that, except for fear, he could hardly tell he was alive. What was he listening for? For silence? Or for a sound in the round of the night, like a point in the compass? There was no rift in the room.

If the dream were a formula, so was the comfort.

'Dollbright doesn't know. The table sold in an auction, twenty-five years ago; it's all past.'

Muttering, he made a light. 'Oh, oh, oh,'he groaned, 'it doesn't work, it doesn't work. He treats me like dirt. I can't bear it. He'll find out. Who, which was that in the street?'

Always murmuring, and occasionally in a very loud voice of which he was unconscious as a deaf man, he got up and moved up and down the room in his dressing gown. He drank water, and rubbed his forefinger against his teeth; one of the most peculiar consequences of the nightmare was the slight but pronounced burning in the tip of this finger, as if it had been used to pinch the wick of a lighted candle.

From a black enamelled cash box he lifted a book; it was full of his own writing. The last read:

'Often, often and now, that most vivid and everlasting minute, when boiling with unnamable remorse, I have cried "perhaps what is in me will be born with this breath, perhaps now it will come out. But this is the one moment which will lighten me. And labouring, clumsy, fear-ridden as I am to the end, up to that very end, there is TIME. The forces groped with black fists in primeval spaces until one chance touched creation. I have not begun. But I have not ended. Chance playings may help me. Time … opportunity…"' To this he added in wild swift writing, like abandoned gestures.

'No. Terrible delusion of Time. Another nightmare. Saw one in the street, the first I have ever met since I was out. Chaos. He will find out, and salvation will be lost. *I must tell*. He will turn me away. To-day he knocked against me on the stairs. If an accident he didn't apologize. What contempt he feels for me!'

Another sentence was scrawled:

'For the tangles and the knots in oneself there are no written rhythms.'

He put the book in his pocket. Then he opened the door, crossed the passage, and softly entered his sister's room, which was opposite his own. Cautiously he examined her by holding the candle level with his shoulder, so that the light fell clear over the high foot of the bed.

Her breath bubbled in the back of her throat. Her open lips had fallen, her head was turned sideways and above the creased sheet showed her sharp collar-bones. The very clothes on her looked withered, and lying flat on her back as she was, a little concave, with her feet crossed, he had a strange impression of a weight crushing her body deep into the mattress.

'Margaret.'

Suddenly she opened her eyes and saw her brother. She moaned, and covered her head.

'Margaret—don't! I won't move. Don't be frightened… I tried not to frighten you.

Margaret!'

She whispered: 'Don't touch me. I m going to die. My heart is stopping.'

'I've come to tell you something.'

She shook, but made not the faintest answer. They had lived before and after one fact. It was always in their minds.

'I'm going to confess to Dollbright. You don't know how I'm tortured! Ah, you do. Dear martyr—'

She stirred as if she were drawing long, hard breaths, and

her foot twitched. It agonized him to see that in her terrified efforts to hide she had pulled the clothes so far over her defenceless head that her feet were naked in the cold.

'I'm still behind the bed. I haven't moved. Let me cover your feet. *No*? Oh my dear, let me, let me.'

She resisted. 'Oh God,' said Benjamin. He stared at the flame. 'I'd better go—'

In a very feeble voice she said: 'Francis will turn you out.'

'Yes, but I can't go on like this. Already he may have heard something. This afternoon I saw someone in the town—one of "those men" edging among the people on the pavement. I'd know his face if a steam roller had been over it. What misery it is! People don't know me. Oh, if you could understand how I want to be known! I'd be easier far, if people ran at me and crushed me against a wall with their thousand bodies. Then I could be honest and feel that they knew me at last, and if I lived after death, I should be in the hands that made me—bad, wretched, wicked! The world's the prison, Margaret. If we could be made afresh and you were not my sister! Don't be terrified, dear. Let me pull the clothes back from your face. You can't breathe. Don't be afraid of me. I'm smashed, wrecked and hopeless.'

'Oh I am frightened! Don't touch me. I'm afraid to look at you.'

'Do you think that I have come to … to—?'

'It comes back to me, too. I never forget even when I'm asleep. Do you want to kill me? I feel as if I were dying. Didn't you come stealing in here tonight to murder me?'

'Oh, Margaret, let me come close to you! Look at me; I have no power to hurt anyone … but *you*, kill you… ? No; every no that's ever been said! I love you beyond all words.'

'You want me to die.'

'Yes I do. I want peace for you.'

'I'm looking forward to dying quietly. Would you choke me?'

'Choke?' repeated her brother wonderingly. He was leaning over the foot of the bed; 'I'd choke myself before I laid a hand on you. How does one choke? Throw back the head in blood and agony, and be gone—on a pillow or a stone, gone away from this. One mustn't waste precious death.'

'It's not you who's going to die.'

'Dear, dear, Margaret, perhaps it is. I'm so tired that I must give way soon.'

She folded her hidden hands.

'Our father which art in heaven,' she said.

'Yes, go on.'

She finished the prayer.

'Amen,' said Benjamin, astray like an idiot who has struck against a word in his untold dumbfoundered world.

'Now light the candle,' moaned Margaret, 'the darkness is too much for me.'

He lit one by her head, and with despair in his sidelong eyes, passed her and went back to his own room. The white muslin curtain was shuddering in the window; a moving cold encircled him, and, as he walked from door to table, and table to bed, a sense of long wandering desolated him, a feeling of being unmoored in this or any life, even by terror.

Why, after all these years, should he wish further to penalize himself?

'Because I have never confessed; because, when I was discovered I fought against the truth. Whatever lawful judge I have faced, not until I learned Dollbright's character, did I find my soul's Judge.'

He sat down at the table and leant on his elbows between piles of books. It must be hard confession to a cruel confessor. And he must speak without premeditation, without extenuation, not in the dark, nor the tender shadow, nor in tottering nightlight. He must not forbid his confession from spreading. He must speak quickly, have his say, and be silent. Then, at last, in him too would be silence.

VI

TWO OBVIOUS factors made the passion of Bellamy Williams for Menna Trouncer interesting to Mill End: one was his occasionally going out with a tall, sallow girl, the daughter of the publican, who was known to be searching for a husband, and the other was Menna's mother.

Mrs. Trouncer was killing herself with whisky. She started her bouts in the bar of the 'Bunch of Grapes', then was seen, torn and grim watching in Mill Street like a jealous dog, for Bellamy to call; and not until she was sop did she retreat to a back room with a skylight, a sofa, and a locked cupboard, the key of which was warm in her bosom. Those were the only times when the pair met at Menna's home.

Perhaps, too, Mill End sensed stranger elements in the affair, beyond the usual courting, a sort of fatal attraction mingled with tragedy. 'Them's the kind of fools that 'ud be found dead in bed with the gas on,' was what was said. Though why…?

Mrs. Trouncer's state seemed obstacle enough to any thoughts of marriage. She hated Bellamy, and such as she could not be left to live alone. The neighbours used to hear her howling for her daughter.

'Are you watching? Don't leave me alone! Don't go down the cellar!' And if she met the young man, witnesses agreed that she glared at him from her yellow eyes until they quailed themselves and prophesied disaster one day to the three. She herself had this foreboding, less clearly, less surely, but more deeply and more wildly, through revelations which vanished into blackness. She would grope with her hands as if to grasp thoughts twisting in the air before her face, and catching at the iron-headed bolt of the door, drag herself upright, aghast at everything. Then, clouding over, she would lower her huge unsound bulk to the sofa again, and sit with her mouth open and her lip shaking, pulling at the lobes of her ears and thinking dimly of the key to oblivion between her breasts. Cruel, greedy love of Menna, and dependence on her were like teeth in the girl; and up and down hard Mill Street, past the shop, on his way to work and back, between the long rooted houses, tramped the relentless Bellamy also pressing his biting need into her flesh. The very sky was a cupping glass. What did they all—Benjamin, Bellamy, her mother, others too, of both sexes—what did they want of her so urgently, but only comfort?

She was a very beautiful young woman, twenty-four years old, strong and pure, with a mouth which was maternally voluptuous. Her neck was very white, shaded pale brown under the hair which touched her shoulders. Her figure was firm yet yielding. Surely her treasures were apparent. Yet she felt that the unloosing of her profoundest instincts would not make her ultimately happy. Nor Bellamy. The world was not her child. She did not pause to think that such children do grow up.

Bellamy was sadistic because he was desperate. By nature rather than intellect he worshipped justice, kindness and truth. The lack of these in Mill End drove him frantic; then he met Menna at the Harmony Club, where he was dancing with Eileen Lewis, and the wardrobe dealer's reserved daughter became the only creature at which his heart refused to point scorn, for all the lashings she dealt it. It seemed as if she held a unique promise for him. She would not admit it. He adored her, and then he nearly hated her for denying him. At first, when he had fallen in love with her, he could forget her. Now he could not. The image of her roused him to hunger and a furious rage. He was obsessed. He worried her like a rag.

'You want to be worshipped,' he accused her venomously. He had a rare and appalling gift of penetration, but with her, except in divining her love for him, he was always wrong. 'Well, I won't worship you, but you're mine.'

'Mother is fond of saying that.'

His bitterness was dreadful. It rent him and it rent her. They fought like tigers, with every cracking sinew. Fiercely she guarded her breast from his touch. His hands she did not fear, but once his head lay there she was caught. And she knew it. And she burned for it. His was a terrible shrivelled wisdom, a crone nursing his young brain between knuckled knees. Existence had flogged and starved him, given him large wants and filed his appetites to arctic keenness. He had thought himself mad. He was a most complete and ravenous human. Professing the most disparaging opinions of our kind, which he classed as pests, frauds or fiends, he was in reality extraordinarily compassionate. He was called up by his nature to help at too many travails.

One night, after Florence had gone to hospital, Menna walked out through the shop and locked the door after her. There were no lights in the house, and Mrs. Trouncer was asleep with her face turned to the wall in the back room.

Menna joined Bellamy at the cross roads. It was raining wildly, and the gutters were awash. They walked rapidly up the hill, leaving Mill End behind them. They were going to the pictures. On the way they spoke only once.

'Are you sure you want to take me?'

'Yes, I am sure. Why should I ask you if I didn't want you?'

'Wouldn't you rather take Eileen Lewis?'

'Oh, hell! No I wouldn't,' said Bellamy, angrily.

'Oh, Bellamy!' she sighed, and paused with a long melancholy look into his eyes. His pale, strange face was bent above her, his gaze hung upon hers with a piercing sadness.

An awful look, not new to Menna. One who remembered many lives might wear it, with eyes on the tireless future. She gasped, and unconsciously knocked her doubled fist upon her breast. In the street as they were he dragged her rigid fingers to his lips and kissed them. They hurried on as if they were possessed or pursued, past the Market House with steps going down into the lighted square, and up the narrow High Street. A row of electric lights glared upon sallow posters, blistered with damp; there was a smell of stone pavement and wet paper, and a group of young fellows, smoking and joking with their hands in their pockets, split to let them pass. Bellamy took the tickets and they entered, just as the picture began. The lights went out. Absentmindedly the operator projected the film upside down. Bellamy cursed. Peeping sideways she caught the glitter of his eyeball. The audience roared and jeered and beat the wooden floor with their feet. The air reeked of freesia scent, the music was so loud it made them feel as if they were inside a drum, being shaken among the files of faces. There was a general expression of numb vacancy, and hands kept rising out of the darkness towards pipes and cigarettes.

Being now accustomed to the dark they turned and once more looked at each other. This time it was a passionate stare of suspense. Suddenly, savagely, Bellamy seized her wrist and stripped the glove off that hand. He held fast to her with twitching fingers.

'Let's go. I want to be with you,' he whispered frantically.

'I want to stay.'

He drew his head away from hers, but continued to clutch her hand against him. They were dreadfully unhappy. Menna was crying, and Bellamy tortured her by abusing her under his breath. His white profile seemed to take on an edge, his lips moved as if he were addressing the leprous enlargements of men in front of him. Towards the end a man quietly carried in a step ladder and, mounting it, opened the long door of the illuminated clock. Stretching up his arm, all the yellow light behind his extended figure, he adjusted the hands. He seemed a saint, who, in the act of blessing this assembly, had turned his back in his niche to indulge in a felonious smile.

'Ha, ha, ha, infallible Time that we go by, there's only a man behind you!' thought Bellamy.

They came out into the street and walked home arm in arm. He asked if he might come in.

'Yes,' she said emptily. She went in front of him into the kitchen, brushing her fur sleeve along the counter as she passed.

A lamp was flaring on the table, with a blackened chimney.

'I didn't leave that!' she exclaimed.

'Menna!' he screamed, beside himself. She turned round shocked to see him stamping on the threshold, as if the doorway were the frame of a rack. He ran to her and turned his arms around her waist, gripping her to him. His teeth showed like hailstones in the storm of his mouth.

'There's nothing you love,' he screamed in the wild voice that was as unnatural to him as strenuous action, and the words rang with a desperation stronger than the glare of his eyes and the grip of his arms. .

'Oh, Menna, Menna, Menna, I'd scarcely be in such despair if I saw you dead or loving another man! Dead you'd be out of chance, and loving would give you substance and a heart which I'd twist towards me. But I can't strain at nothing, and nothing is all I've got to beg you by. What do you hold to? What can't you spare when you've spared everything? What's your most inner and last hope? I'll pray and implore you by that to take me and love me… love me. I want the looks that you hide from me, the time that you spoil, all the joys that you kill and keep back. I want my sleep from you, my life, my rest. I'm deserted and sleepless without you. I want your hands on my head—it's all pain and longing! Take me, Menna darling, dear love—' Tightly as he held her, forcing her face close to his own with his hard right hand over her ear and his gasps crossing her lips, she scarcely felt the pressure on her living body. But each word melted her. She looked at him, lifted her hand and put it against his neck; then her eyes yielded, and his own name seemed uttered in them rather than in sound. Neither would move; they were walled up in passion, in a rigid pause, a stricken knowledge of what was inevitable between them. All softness and elasticity departed, even the tremulousness of breathing. Their eyes were like callouses. At last he spoke, but with indescribable difficulty, as though something bolted and barred within him were making noises behind a door.

'Now … is it… love?'

She could not answer, could do nothing but gaze while her hand began to stir on his neck and she learned the line of his lips forever.

'If we two part,' he toiled on in the same weak, yet urgent tone, 'we shall always hanker after each other. You'll never forget me; I have burned into you.'

'Yes—'

In a desperate spasm they simultaneously clutched each other and stood blind and reeling with their faces stricken together. Then the strength ran out of them. Bellamy fell against the wall, covering his eyes, and Menna sank down on the floor at his knees.

And then they suffered an interruption. For one second they thought the whole of the window which gave on the inner yard had crashed inwards. Glass lay shivered on the stone floor, catching the light of the flaring lamp in flashing splinters, and through the centre pane, transfixing, it seemed, light and outer darkness like an untrembling axis, was the arm of Mrs. Trouncer and her bloody fist. Nothing else of her was visible.

'Oh, God, what has she done?' said Bellamy aghast, his sick face turned immovably upon the slowly relaxing limb.

'Quick,' Menna shouted, snatching the lamp, 'she's falling—she'll cut the artery. Come and hold her up!'

She rushed out, the lamp streaming light and disarrayed shadows across the ceiling. He followed. Menna had stood the lamp upon the ground. The bulk of the drunken woman was leaning sideways on the window ledge—like something draining. He shuddered.

'Thank God the cellar trap was shut!' Menna exclaimed.

'*Thank God?*' he questioned … fiercely. Between them they supported her ponderous weight, and drew the arm back. Only the knuckles were cut. The mottled flesh was slack and wet. She was grimacing. Her face hung lolling, on her shoulder, weighted and sagging sideways; she stretched her mouth in a grin, her wild and dabbled hair smothered her ears.

Supporting her, Bellamy felt sick. He was afraid he would retch from the odious proximity of her flesh. She was heaped upon him. Why didn't something fall on her, crush her, end her, put her out of their way! Wicked and damnable creature who interposed Menna between herself and her twisted visions, who would stagger drunk to her deathbed—go soon, go soon…

As they lurched towards the door he looked up at the craning roof and the froth of stars. The wind wheeled around the house, around the light that Menna carried. A skein of black smoke streamed from the sooty glass, winding like her hair. Piling his miserable curses on the interruption, panting and struggling, and stopping now and again to rest against the wall, he got Mrs. Trouncer into the house. Menna ran to help him, and between them they brought her to the small room at the back, and guided her to the sofa. Bellamy stood back against the wall wiping his hands on his sides. He could have kicked and hit her. The sweat broke out on him. It was so hot in the close little room with its low ceiling and shut window. An earthenware cup was lying smashed on the hearth among the dead cinders, and he noticed the gleam of spilt liquid.

Menna pulled off her mother's shoes and dropped them on the floor. Mrs. Trouncer rolled over on her face, one arm dangling over the edge of the sofa, groaning. The girl fetched a basin of warm water and rags and tried to wash the cut hand, but the woman kept it obstinately clenched beneath her. When Bellamy attempted to touch her she lifted her head and poured curses on them both through a mouthful of hair: 'Keep your—fingers off me or I'll bite 'em off.'

'Then let her be!' said Menna, getting up frrom her knees, 'let her stay in here in the dark and dream as she deserves! She's not hurt. Come out, Bellamy.'

She seized his wrist and dragged him after her, shutting the door. The whole place reeked of lamp smoke, a draught from the broken pane cut the kitchen in half.

'How she *must* dream!' he gasped, crouching away from the sounds into the furthest corner of the settle.

'She does! She dreams and fears and hates all at once; and all day and night now. Dreams! You'd think there was someone in there murdering her. There listen—she's banging on the floor!'

She started up, her hands suspended in the air, her white wrinkled lips moving. Mrs. Trouncer was screaming, groaning and thumping on the door. After a silence she began to shout as if in a brawl; filthy abuse and the utmost rage were mingled with sobs, groans and bumps; it resounded all along the passage.

'It's awful … awful. Don't go to her, Menna!' She turned a dark look on him: 'I *brought her here.* '

Suddenly her reserve ended in passionate confession. She flung herself away from his touch and hid her face from him against the wall.

'Oh, Bellamy, leave me alone, leave me here as I was before I knew you! I pray she'll die, and I don't care how. It's not my fault she's drinking but it is that we're here together. I can't stop her, though I used to try—now let her kill herself not me … not me,' she wailed groping in her hair.

'She didn't want to leave Salus. She and my uncle used to go it together after Dad died, drank whisky by the pailful and hid it everywhere. I've found it under a stone in the yard! They sat hand in hand, and auntie used to come and sit in the house and wait for them. Oh, Bellamy, Bellamy, if you'd seen it all! Bottles under the mattress, and mother lying on top of them till we tried to draw them out from underneath, then she'd sit up and give a laugh at us both. This went on and on for days; auntie was like a fiend raging everywhere—'

'Menna!'

'I'd have done anything to end it. I said I would. I said I'd be with her anywhere if she'd only come away. Do you think I would now? No; she *shall* kill herself. I don't so much as hide the drink when I find it. *I'd like to get it for her*. Do you know what she said to me? She said she'd rather put a light to me when I was asleep and burn me up than see me with you.'

'Menna, Menna, bring me a candle!' shouted Mrs. Trouncer. Menna snatched a candle with a vindictive smile. Bellamy sprang to her, pulled it out of her hand, and threw it down. He grasped her arms with desperate strength above the elbows and they swayed and struggled face to face and eye to eye.

'Wrench away if you can,' said he; 'you're not going while I have strength to keep you back or a breath to lose! *I* love you. I need you, *I'm* better worth the saving. *She* tortures herself, she has only one devil; but I can't escape from legions without you. You're mine—you *must* be, or add to my agony.'

Menna stood still, panting, her eyes straining over some spiritual threshold; he hid his face in her neck under her ear. He stroked her hair along his forehead. He would never die out of her now; all the promises she had ever made would be lost in that she would give him. The light furrowed her brows. The taut minutes passed. She was mute, horrified, almost senseless. When he released her she sat down, thrust her hands between her knees and stared at the kettle as if it were the end of the world perched on perdition. The tears ran down each side of her nose, she clenched her teeth. He began to think she would never speak again.

Kneeling beside her he tried to caress her.

'Speak to me.'

'I can't.'

'Say that you'll marry me!'

'I can't promise you.'

Bellamy got up from the floor.

'You won't leave her even though she's killing herself and I'm struggling to live?'

'I can't promise,' she repeated,

'Good-bye,' he said almost inaudibly.

'Bellamy!'

'Yes.'

'Give me a month!'

'Give me a life.'

'Oh, Bellamy, do come to me!'

He stared at her as one who is watching something disappear and pronounced with extraordinary deliberation; 'I will always say good-bye to you.'

Then he went.

For every minute of the next hour she expected him to return, as he had always. But he did not. She walked round and round the kitchen, her mouth hanging open, her fists pressed against her temples. He was her affliction. She seemed to draw breath over a red-hot bar in her breast. She stood in a rage of love. She trod agony. Would the windows never show dawn? The heavens were paved with winds; the rain scratched at the glass, like nails. Her mother's voice, subdued now, glimmered along the passage. She lay asleep, a candle on the table beside her throwing a shadow on the wall like a range of mountains. At one o'clock the policeman was adjured to 'get them cursed rag-pickers to fasten their bloody door, or he, Harry Brooks, would open up their faces from mouth to ear in the morning.' The policeman turned slowly and focused a wild face peering down at him from the house opposite the Trouncers. The band of a nightshirt cut the base of the neck off short. This man was an old enemy of Mrs. Trouncer. On more than one occasion she had fought him blow for blow, and Mill End still talked of the day when she had tried to batter in his door with a hatchet.

The policeman ordered him to keep quiet and then entered the house. Menna was sitting on the fender in the kitchen. The window was smashed, the lamp sooty, the wind playing on the hearth, the rafters black as Blackie Gwyre.

'Anything wrong, Miss?'

'Nothing,' she said drowsily, if drowsiness can result from a preoccupation other than sleep.

'Your street door's not fastened.'

She followed him silently, locked it after him, and then stood in the shop clasping her hands under her chin until the nails were numb from pressure. She had no thoughts. Presently she returned and lay down on the settle. Just before dawn the lamp went out. And the darkness thinned and morning was blown along the street like a white shadow. Bellamy passed. The syren sounded, the workers shook off the night. The troll of the Mill set his belts whirling and his steam flying. The light swooped from the hills to the roofs and from them to the faces of the men binding their vague proportions within hard outlines; the darkness sank through the earth, through stone and pavements and down trodden ways, to a hidden well.

Morning went over. About noon a hand appeared in front of the red curtain in the Trouncers' shop window and propped up a card with the word 'CLOSED' printed on it. Such a thing had never been before; it was another sign of the rot inside, and provoked immense speculations.

That night was the last time Gwen Trouncer was ever seen drunk in the street. Without a coat, aiding herself by a flapping umbrella, she lurched across the road and began bellowing at Brooks. He was sober and magnanimous. He took her by the scuff of the neck, pushed her into the shop and threw her down under the counter like a stuffed sack, observing:

'You're more like a wild beast than a woman.'

Even he thought her terrible.

In her scrubby dirty dress, the bodice undone, her hair brushed up from her forehead by the violent sweeping of her arm, she lay gasping, her tongue out of her mouth. Her eyes floated like foul bubbles on her ghastly face; she clasped her hands on the top of her head as if to squeeze it down into her body. Then she put out her hand, and clinging to the edge of the counter, dragged herself on to her knees. Her lips stretched and revealed each separate decaying tooth in the yellow gums—oh, it was horrible to think that such a spirit as showed then in those swollen surfaces ever had been young, or happy or innocent and peaceful, under a covering of youth! An old mind will watch from young eyes, and childishness play in palsy, but *here* age looked older than itself, older than being has right or claim to be, on earth among frailty. Such looks were burned, such wisdom was cut off because something in the possessors had matured beyond life and beyond the farthest boundaries of sanctioned cultivation. These people are the witches, the Fausts, the wandering Jews, the devil-pledged souls, the makers of thralls and curses, whose formulas bring fear and evil even in the worn uncomprehending repetition.

As a wave will wrinkle up in the sea the fury mounted in her eyes. She gabbled and coughed and hissed with hatred. Brooks ran out of the shop. She fell backwards on the flags, her legs drawn sideways, a garter hanging in a loop from her ankle.

'They'll tear the life out of me … they'll watch me dying—'

With a howl she attempted once more to lift herself, but the counter was beyond her grasp and she fell back again.

Menna came in with a light. She stooped, held it close to her mother's face and pronounced distinctly: 'Suppose I set fire to *you*? You can't stop me …*you* can't move.'

After this, Mrs. Trouncer was afraid of her. She took to drinking in her bedroom, having locked the door. Menna listened to the sounds. Sometimes, when she thought she was alone, she sat at the head of the stairs, her arm twined in and out of the balustrade, peering down between the railings for a sight of her daughter. If she saw her she tottered back to her room, either cursing or wailing that all the world ought to pity her. She wept as loudly as she shouted, and her voice could be heard in the street at the dead of night:

'Menna, Menna, come to your Mammy! Fetch a light. I'm stuck … my tongue's gone down my gullet. You can't bury me … I'm not dead yet ' . .

There are many, I know, who by this time will have picked up this book and put it down again. Having opened it, perhaps, read a page or two, they will pass their usual comment.

'Why write about such people?'

I wish they would read to the end. Maybe they would find a line of their own likeness, though no one is in my mind as I draw it. I own that *I* am here.

True I have chosen to write of the people of Mill End, and not those of Lindenfield. The former stands at the bottom, the latter at the top, of the hill upon which Chepsford is built. And whether you examine towns or tubs, human, animal or atmospheric nature, you will always find the dregs at the bottom.

But what are the dregs if they are not the essence of the whole?

The stars are the lees of space. The earth itself is a mote. Seas are rocked in dust.

I have never read any books on theology; but I have heard what I thought was God's voice in strange mouths. I have heard his name sound wonderful and holy in a furious row outside the pub, and I have heard sanctified congregations worshipping literature.

As for God—imaginations have bestowed the power and the glory upon him, but in fact he has only his name. He is like a madman, whose property very truly is his, only he is not allowed to make use of it. And like a madman is God in that to manifest his strength, he has to break through the restraining bonds of those very ones who declare his calamitous might, and fear his fires.

No. It requires not Christ to symbolize the poverty of God. It is so evident! With half the world pouring divinity on his altars, with all the building and decking of his houses, the painting of his revelations, he is still only a word among worse words.

His kingdom on earth is in oaths and men's deaths and despairs. He is in every man's mouth, though he die with each one. Wherever there's shame and cruelty and wickedness, tongues drag him in as the one thing that can stand up to them—he is preached in all the sins and proclaimed in curses.

To return to the Dollbrights... .

Florence had no relapse; from the first she strode towards recovery. She believed that it was a cyst which had been taken from her, and that belief restored her religious complacence after the first week of sickness and groaning.

To her husband she spoke of trials to be endured for the Lord's sake, of the efficacy of prayer, and the steadfastness of faith. She sent a message by him to the minister, and when he came in answer to it, requested him to pray aloud for herself and her husband and for everybody else in the ward and their husbands.

Mr. Tielard demurred; but ended by offering up a general prayer and then went round the beds and shook hands with all the embarrassed and interrupted conversationalists.

Once Dollbright met the minister at the hospital; the encounter was no more than a moment and a murmur across the bed, but Florence watched them both with keen interest. If Francis would join the Baptists! Surely Mr. Tielard was the very man to persuade him. Dollbright was only conscious of a sudden irritation against his wife and her visitor with the white cravat, the block of hair over each ear, and the careful voice.

The minister held out his fingers. Dollbright gave them a merciless screw, hoping it hurt. These days he lived in rigid outline, strangely accustomed to the mere forms of his existence. His desk...his table...his bed...the hospital... Day after day piled up between him and his vow. He was placed against set scenery.

However, one Sunday an experience befell him which afterwards affected his attitude towards Benjamin Wandby.

He walked into the country, following a path along the railway which led into the fields. He turned while he was still in sight of the town and looked back at it. The Mill chimney sprang from the sluttish scramble of roofs, the rubbish dump smoked. There was something careless and akimbo about this aspect of Chepsford. It resembled a back door thronging with businesslike but genial company. He went on. Around him spread the fields tempered by a grey sky.

He could not consider Florence as an example of the 'steadfastness of faith.' There had been too many varieties in her moods. Gradually depression dragged his head down upon his breast. He descended to river level and pursued his way for some distance beside it; at one point he stopped and stood upon the verge staring and listening until his ears were dull and his sight jammed by the lure of the flow. He grew rigid as a monument over the place where he had died…

The river, the river, the river!

Willows dived into the water. A bird dropped from the sky among the branches. It made solitude.

Suddenly Dollbright shook his fist in front of him. The gesture stood out against the current like a solid bar in a molten stream. Then he moved slowly away. He felt an awful weakness come over him and knew that he must lie down. He looked helplessly at the slimy sheep track under his feet, and the dreary wet field around him. His feet slithered, his eyes wandered in vague distance till they came to rest on a barn about a quarter of a mile away on the rising side of a hill. It was an answer.

When he came up to it he discovered that one great door was ajar, the base being buried in muck and immovable. He squeezed through the aperture.

The interior was at first no more than a dusk inside the dusk outside. He seemed to sink into it, and into the smell of roots and old hay. It was a dank, sour earthy smell. After some time he could distinguish the form of some bony machinery with a still and secret wheel, and a sort of loft reached by a ladder lacking several rungs. He climbed it and lay down on a small heap of hay. The rest of the flooring was of rough rat-bitten boards, and a draught crossed it from the opposite slits in the walls.

The shapes below him seemed to be taking a grim rest. He realized that he was afraid, then that he was terrified. He shut his eyes. The wheel began to turn under his eyelids, but it was bright and the thick spokes threw out showers of atoms in patterns that kept changing.

'I'm a long way from home,' he said, 'am I afraid to go back?'

He knew that it was not the barn which was working on his fear, but the idea of going home.

Mr. Tielard's voice seemed to speak in his ear: 'You know ministers have privileges,' it repeated mincingly over and over again. In the centre of the floor upon which he was prone was a hole or trap about three feet square, black like a well, and directly above it a strong beam. He stared from the beam to the hole, from the hole to the beam. A design for death!

Hang, hang… the giddy notion of it filled him. It rose from unconsciousness to plain reality. He sat up. Let him take his life and swing above the dark until the morning.

When the wheel began to work and the slits admitted

cobwebby light, they would look up to the rafters and there would be evening which would not wait upon day…

A long time passed. He stood twisting his handkerchief into a line, a creature in a balance, not tragic, not defiant or passionate, but blank and witless, without a word of grief. It was now too dark in the barn to distinguish his upright figure standing in the almost bare loft midway between the ground and roof. He might have been hanging. Or tying the rope. Or breaking his vow and praying before he jumped. Or covering his eyes.

The warped door moaned as a man pushed through it. He took a lantern from a hook on the wall and sat down on the bottom of the ladder, gripping it between his legs and prying into it with a lighted match. He whistled between his teeth. Presently, having adjusted the wick, he went out, waving the lantern so that a swinging-boat of light rocked upon the sandstone wall, and rendered to the wheel a semblance of soundless turning. He was gone. The light and the shadows were gone as if they had jumped into a box and been shut down. A strange harsh noise, from no direction, pierced the void stillness —a noise of gasping and weeping, the shaking of a loose board. No words, but again and again the terrifying strangling sobs as if grief and life were choking in a noose. Then it stopped. There was a heavy bending footfall on the ladder, and the barn was delivered of Dollbright's presence. He stumbled into the field with his hand to the side of his face, as if his sight had been stricken by the inert sway of a body. The barn was more horrible to him than any place he had ever been in. It was like a dreadful impulse which had burst outside his brain without harming him, but settled on the hillside to wait. He fled, feeling it behind him. It was the hour when all the farm dogs wail over dusk. There was a wild perspective in the clouds, the earth was black and solid to the tops of the trees, which stood all around and round him like the rim of a concave disc. But the sky seemed perpendicular and light stood upright in the west, like a giant in armour far along a fading aisle.

The man was terrified as in nightmare. It was a long time since darkness had come upon him in the open, and the walls of his mind were razed. In the streets it was more sudden and precipitate, a black waterfall in the gorge; one minute the lamps were unlit and the next... .

But here it was so gradual and remorseless, a drowning in blindness. He felt that he was running down an open throat, that he could not bear it if the sky too closed upon his eyes and squeezed him between two meeting masses. He kept shutting and opening his eyes to mark the increase of darkness—it was darker—it was not —he could not tell. Everything shouted a louder life, a soulless fearlessness, an unchanged continuity, a solitary inhumanity, and he had no hearth in his thoughts!

He went along by the river, not running, but panting and striving after pace. It seemed to be pouring a ceaseless volume of water into a tunnel. The trees shivered as if no sun had ever touched them. The reeds and grasses were secret as a jungle. The wind was the only breath upon creation. The earth nursed it close, then it bounded from the lap and ran along the rim rapping a regiment of drums. Then it died, and the air drooped like a black flag from the heights. Drops of rain fell on his face. The porches of the west caved in, smouldered and went black beneath the low driving clouds. He scudded before them. A mile, two miles were passed, his hands were wet, his forehead swollen. Now when he looked back he saw nothing but an entire blackness out of which he had come. It was incredible that he had been *there* alone and not gone mad with terror. Before him he saw the lights of Chepsford.

When at last he crossed his own doorstep he was reeling. He sank down on the lowest stair in the hall with his head on his hands. That sky….that earth abandoned by light and rolling eternally…

He tried to think. But he had reached the stage of fear, fear, and only fear. The utmost ghastliness of which his brooding imagination was capable was short of what death must be, if he fell between God's unretaining knees. If he must perish…

And he must.

From that hour he forsook solitude and clung to the fireside. He did not talk. He was not amiable or communicative, and the lines of his face and forehead were tragic and lowering. He settled into his chair, his hands knotted; his gaze unsettled, wandering and hungry, sucked in the insignificant details of the room, the shadows on the ceiling and the sinister transformation which distance and a bad light lent to the two conventional steel engravings over the door. After one or two evenings spent in this unnatural staring his attention was gradually weaned from objects towards Benjamin Wandby.

He was a restless, though silent, companion. In and out a dozen times in the course of an evening, he would enter with his eyes fixed on Dollbright as if he were only awaiting the signal of a smile to start a conversation; it never came. Dollbright did not want Benjamin's friendliness; he hated him. All he wished was to feel a consciousness other than his own in the room, to have, which he felt he had, a fellow sufferer. He wanted to forget his agonizing sense of marked isolation. He began to study Benjamin.

They were queer, the things he noticed, the things he wrapped around his importunate ideas. His mind worked incessantly, spinning cobwebs of dreary conjecture. He watched Benjamin sitting close to the table, his body leaning forward upon one elbow, his other hand grasping the newspaper under the lamp, his head tilted against the sombre wallpaper. He had a receding forehead; the base of his head was no longer than normal; so Dollbright asked himself, 'had Wandby less brain than the ordinary, or was it dangerously compressed? and what actions or thoughts lay imbedded in that narrow compass? What distortions and deformities harried his mind? How did *his* mental images wriggle in their pent-house?'

And then his eyes…why did he look at one so long, so enigmatically, and sigh, and relinquish his slight occupations? What was the inward object to which his gaze returned, and plunged and rose again like a diver, loaded?

These questions provoked answers as vague and fantastic as the shapes and likenesses which a sick man discovers in the cracks of a ceiling. Florence's return was to take place the day after to-morrow. It was a Sunday evening, about six o'clock. Dollbright and Benjamin were both in the front room. The fire was poor, the lamp, placed in the middle of the large red mahogany table, shone again in the window above the net curtains. Benjamin, with arms thrown above his head and legs bent under his chair, looked as if he were recalling some painful experience; and he was.

Earlier in the day he had gone to his bedroom to get a book. Menna was sweeping the floor on her knees, with the soles of her feet turned upwards and her hair hiding her face in its folds. Benjamin felt a glow of desire as he watched her, pretending, as he did so, to search among the papers on the table. He felt again the sensation of helpless attraction…the certainty of folly, and he shrank as he recalled the things that he had done.

'But if the miracle had happened?' he thought, and flushed with stolen delight which merciless fact derided. 'Ah!'

'Have you been looking at any of my papers?' he had asked. He saw her stand up holding her brush, and heard her angry reply:

'Of course I haven't. I'm not a spy!' After another pretence of examining them he made her a slight bow and held out his hand.

'Forgive me.'

Without saying anything more, and without remembering how he did it, he took hold of her greedily.

'Oh, you're lovely,' he muttered in a throttled voice as if he were weeping, 'I want to kiss you so badly!'

Her body seemed to change from luxury to desolation in his arms. He loosened her and let her go while a dreadful shame of his age and clumsiness made him incapable of words. She picked up her brush which had fallen on her foot.

'You ought to say you're sorry, Mr. Wandby,' she said coolly.

'I am; very sorry. I make you a profound apology. You're a wise child, wiser than your years, Menna. You see … it was only for a moment I was overcome. You are so beautiful! There's a shadow on your neck under your hair that would make any old man a fool. Forget it if you can.'

'Oh yes, I can forget it.'

He smiled despairingly—it was so true! And then his pitiful admission that he was desperate. At once he snatched it back.

'I've frightened you again. Rubbish, Menna, don't take any notice of what I say. Listen—d'you know there's one very merry old chap in Chepsford, and that's myself.'

Benjamin brought his arms to his sides and moved his head from side to side against the back of the chair as though he were in pain. He felt accursed; his memory was foul like a pond which no fresh water purges, which was bottomed with slime. His slightest recollections were unpleasant; the greatest of them was terrible. It never left him for long; as he looked at Dollbright a qualm went through him, and with a sudden involuntary groan he got up and went out of the room.

The Salvation Army was marching past the house. The glass in the windows trembled with the tread, the drum seemed to throb in the walls. Behind, among a small crowd stalked the newly converted Viking with raindrops in his moustache. The women's faces were limp with an expression of colourless patience. Their destination was the market place where they would stand singing in the rain, the lights hovering on their brass instruments. For a little while after they were gone Dollbright's thoughts followed the door to door lives of these people, then leaning forward on his knees he took up the poker, and began drawing the point through the ashes. He wrote:

'Florence.'

And beneath it:

'Faith.'

He scratched the poker raspingly against the hearth-stone with a sound which put one's teeth on edge, and scattered the warm ashes in dust upon the fender. A savage hatred of all his circumstances, and a lust to take revenge on everybody and everything made him hurl the poker at the wall. It fell with a dull clang; Dollbright leaped up, jammed his hat on his head and went out. While he was walking his mood changed, or rather burned afresh with the same inspiration like one flame lighted from another.

When he returned he went to find Benjamin. He was in his workroom sitting in the armchair and looking at the palms of his hands, which were open on his knees like a book. He got up laboriously. His pockets sagged baggily, his legs shook beneath the weight of his heavy body, his colour was ghastly. He picked up the candle and held it in both hands against his chest, and the draught blew the light along one side of his face and over his shoulder where it dispersed in the shadows behind him.

'Ah, Mr. Dollbright, I was going to ask for a little of your company to-night! Will you stay with me a moment or two?'

Having said this he seemed like a man overcome by terror who does not know what will happen to him. His jaw trembled and he leaned upon the table as if he were going to faint.

'Sit down, damn you!'

'You hate me, don't you? Don't you, don't you?' Benjamin gabbled. His eyes and Dollbright's drew gradually nearer and nearer, yet there was no collision of gaze. Rather Dollbright's stare ran itself into a mist which there was no withstanding. For the first time in his life he looked *outwards* at suffering, and he saw—himself.

Almost supernaturally disturbed he stared at Benjamin's remote eyes in a kind of wild alarm. He was talking madly, it seemed as if he had lost control of himself but held it fixed upon an external point.

'Your wife is coming home to-morrow, isn't she? That makes it my last evening, because she *might* take my part. I want no allies. You are free, quite free to repeat what you like, remember that. No!...Margaret...I must ask you to treat this as a confidence, as a confession.'

'A confession.'

'Yes. Or a defiance. I defy you. You hate me—'

'Yes, I do!'

'You hate me, and I am afraid of you. I am a coward and yet I defy you! It does not take a god to defy you, Dollbright— only a coward who has been in torment for fifteen years, ever since he met you and knew your character.'

'Sit down, sit down, you lunatic,' shouted Dollbright leaning across the candlestick and trying to force Benjamin into a chair.

'You're my judge—' stammered Benjamin and he flung off Dollbright's arm. Their fighting shadows locked upon the ceiling. They saw the walls and the floor at a staggering angle; their feet shuffled among the corkscrew shavings from the lathe. The candle-flame bent, pointed towards Benjamin's heart as overcome he sank into the chair.

'God is your judge,' Dollbright gasped.

'Since when have *you* left that to Him? Arch-angel, do your duty!'

'You are out of your senses. What do you want to tell me?'

There was a pause like a fuse burning… Benjamin spoke:

'Twenty-seven years ago I tried to murder my sister. I was in prison for five years out of the seven of my conviction.'

When he had spoken he smiled and put his hand on his eyes to hide his tears.

Dollbright lurched towards him, holding the candle at the level of his chin.

'That's true?'

'Quite true.'

He replaced the candle on the table. The dusty barn, the wheel and the trap-door—would-be murderer and would-be suicide in one light…

'What right have you to tell me this? Never speak of it again. Never. What else that's ghastly have I in my house to break on me? Weeks ago I thought my wife was well, my living good, and you a quiet man growing old. Now I hate my work, despise myself, my wife has cancer, you are a criminal, and I have been tempted to kill myself. God has hidden from me! Destruction is the root of everything!'

And he repeated, staring into the windings of the future:

'Never speak of it again. Never mention your private life to me again.'

'I have to live,' said the other trembling.

'So have I,' cried Dollbright, 'why tell me? Am I to carry your sins on my sore feet? Are you to sleep while I wake, take coin from me to buy off your conscience? I tell you this … I have not heard you!'

'Aren't you going to turn me out?'

'A week, two days ago, yes I would. But not now. Where would you fit in half so well as you do here?'

*

The mirror gleamed, Benjamin could not tell from what reflection of light. He carried none.

He lay down on the bed.

Would all men stone one another? He thought so. Hatred came of the rare glimpse. If one could only foster hatred! But no, it waned and left one desolate on the tide mark.

In the world there must be still many, many faces which he knew horribly well, knew like a lesson, like an affliction, like a disease. They were the faces of the men who had been in prison with him and pursued him with an implacable harmony. He belonged to their memory. And if he met them no change of years would have altered their features; he would recognize their skulls.

A dogged company. Over what a diversity of looks these memories spread! In the prison—he would never forget it— they used to fall staringly upon a new man, squeeze out all his news, stare at him, drink him in, devour his appearance, his strangeness, his difference from themselves, even sniff at him because free air had lately blown upon his skin and in his hair; then disgusted by the maddening staleness that so rapidly overtook him, cruelly drop him and sink back in their grey pining.

Of all the things in the prison this was the worst. Of all its results this was the uneffaceable.

He had been punished not by years but by a lifetime, and his sentence had still to run.

Was it winter clouds that made the rooms so dark? The hospital where he had been once or twice was light and clear, sterilized by effort to a pure worldly cleanliness which bitterly contrasted with this overcast resentful house. The three inhabitants, Dollbright, himself and Margaret moved, sat, united and separated in almost pauseless silence, each staring inward, wide as wind, at their own row of reckonings. It seemed as if their slow feet left mouldy tracks and they were less living than returning to death. All, all within sight had to pass through their sullen eyes and lost its parts of joy.

*

Peace first came to him in a dream. But awakening held it.

*

Dollbright avoided Benjamin after the scene in the work-room.

Often, the following day at the shop, he stopped and looked through the small murky panes of the window, or strolled to the door to watch the spurts of smoke from the station going up into the sky.

The Viking, kneeling on the top of his ladder with his brush swooping in a half circle at the end of his arm, indicated a poster showing a huge pint of beer, and hailed him with his loud untroubled yell from the masthead of existence:

'Hey, a bit o' that's what *you* want!'

'Who're you to talk? You've given all that up since you joined the Salvation Army,' Dollbright retorted.

The Viking spat, and looked away, looked again, and winked his unconverted eye.

But Dollbright's forehead was like a fall of rocks.

VII

THE LAST chapter, the drawing of conclusion around one like a robe, how difficult it is!

That afternoon Dollbright rang up the hospital to find out what time to fetch Florence. They said 'at once;' he called a taxi and went. As he entered the hospital she was coming down the stairs with the matron, a nurse carrying her suitcase.

'Oh, Frank…!' she said, holding out her two long, thin arms towards him. Yet she seemed to belong to them rather than to him, and to the hospital rather than her home. She seemed to be passing out from familiarity to strangeness. The past was inverted.

As Dollbright climbed after her into the taxi he saw the green lawn, the line of villas in the distance, the nesting branches and the starry glimpses of the sun, all the minutiae of the wind blowing on the short blades of grass. The matron stood under the porch, her hands clasped, her elbows jutting from her sides. His only feeling was one of dull astonishment and confusion. His tongue was heavy, his thoughts gabbled in his head. Florence's face was reflected in the black patch on the glass made by the driver's back. It looked terrible, ghostly, as though the light were eating it away.

Men in black hats were standing near the entrance of the Baptist Chapel. 'As soon as I'm well enough I shall go and give thanks,' said Florence. A boy was selling papers outside their own front door, and Benjamin's face was to be seen in the window under the bird-cage. He smiled as if delighted to see Florence come home, ran and opened the house to them. They went in. Dollbright drew a long deep sigh.

*

Mill Street ran roughly west, so that at a certain time in the afternoon the sun threw the shadows of roofs and chimneys on the faces of the opposite houses. This only happened in winter.

It was a long, sloping street, rather narrow, having the mill at one end and the grey gas-works at the other. Many of the hovels were condemned but had not yet been vacated; they were old, filthy and terribly dilapidated with thick, grimy plaster peeling off the walls, laths peeping through gaps like bones through rotting flesh, and smashed windows bunged up with sodden newspaper. Hanging porches were propped up by posts, hollowed steps sheered into dark holes; poisoned rats glided up and down the pavements at night looking for water, and swarmed in the drain-pipes at the side of the road which was worn and rough with flints and loosened stones. The lamps flared on the broken windows, the wind careered with rubbish in the low-roofed alleys while the people played the concertina, drank, fought and lay down on the pavements with their caps over their faces and grit in their verminous hair. The women wore their skirts hitched up in layers round their waists, and men's boots when men had done with them: their husbands showed blue dickies on a Sunday and gorgeous silk scarves instead of collar or tie on other days. The children wore dirt and what was left over, and played such games as the law allowed outside. And all, all teemed with unabated vitality. Furtive, gnawing scraps of food, contemptuous and threatening, they peered from the cracks between the houses or shrieked across the road. They graced neither church nor chapel, but hence the Salvation Army drew those great voices which soared on Market Hill, those lungs which filled the trumpet's mouth and blew music over the prostrate roofs, those powerful arms which beat the drum to bursting. They were a strong, hardy, savage lot, unsated and vindictive: the men looked callous and sulky, the women were spitfires with razor elbows and mad hair. Thus in their youth: but they died young or lived into a vile old age like their own scabby hovels. And there were no town councillors to condemn their worn out carcasses, exchange their tumbling ruins for upright limbs, and lay on clean blood from the main. More's the pity. Even their architectural enterprises were stillborn: a new suburb became a new slum, only a narrow stream of time flowed between the two. The dirt filtered back where it belonged. Chepsford scorned its squalid children—dirt's place is underfoot.

Halfway up Mill Street was an old disused churchyard without a church. No more dead were carried there. The living came instead and sat under the ignoble walls and looked at the trellis of the stars or the day sky unravelling. Long ago grief had gone away to heal itself. Looking on this deserted dust was a block of five cottages, old but still pretty sound, and in the first of these Bellamy Williams lived with his foster-mother, the policeman's wife. The policeman had died four years back, but his widow drew two pensions, and Bellamy paid her eighteen shillings a week out of his thirty. A street lamp on a queerly-twisted bracket protruded over the door and lighted up the steps at night. On the far side was a tall house whose broken, perpetually open sash windows lent it an air of deplorable misery. Quick to fasten on anything ugly or sad, Bellamy's morbid thoughts had haunted the empty house from childhood up. At first he was proud of the way his wild fancies would stare at him from those glass-jagged window frames and withdraw into the untrodden darkness of the rooms; but growing older and more desperate to escape from himself, he hated it and longed to see daylight on its site.

A week or two after his last parting with Menna he went home after work, refused to eat anything, and lighting a candle, went up to his bedroom. He was in a frightful state of mind. At night his bed grew hot with passion, he could not sleep, he was ill and he had no comfort. Between feverish desire and cantankerous bitterness he was burning away. Around his eyes were purple shadows, his mouth was like a crack in ice, his thin hands were always clutching something. He was mute. He knew he must have a woman, and because Menna wanted him near her yet would not marry him or take him in to her, he distrusted her, scorned her and bewitched her image into the demon of his visions. His suffering attained torture. He writhed from side to side in his chair as the terrible enchanting throes of love roused him. Every nerve felt a shock of delight, only to be numbed the next moment by the voice of his clear intellect saying 'It's hopeless.'

Pale, quivering, cursing, he sat there. His leg twitched and above his eye he felt a sharp throbbing of neuralgia. As all sensation seemed knotted upon that one nerve in his forehead, so Menna beat on his heart. He remembered the first time he had danced with her at the Harmony Club, her bare back under the full flood of electricity. He had kissed her back: she was so preoccupied that she had not even known it was his mouth

which had touched her. He would never be free of the goad!
If she wouldn't marry him she would divorce him from
marriage… there was truly a predestined element in their love,
a single deadly attraction which, melting every other tie,
makes living apart a despairing loneliness, and which brings
with it the only full and true dread of death at its most awful,
separation from each other.

His was a life panting with gasps of love, reduced by
scarcity to passion. All that he wanted before he died was to
be in her arms pressed up to her mouth. Ah, how should he
ever die out of her! There were moments when he had
thrown himself at her knees, choked for her like breath,
fought to retain her like life blood … then she was gone. It
was dark—he glanced out and saw shadows clubbed on the
road, groups welded together shouting and kicking the
stones along the gutters. He could have thrown up his head
and howled into the roof. Did she think of him now? By God
and murdered Christ, was he to live in her thoughts? Rot
them. Oh God, he hated something—himself, her. He would
not count his time between glimpses of his darling. A day
was twelve hours. A night was twelve hours. Throbbing,
sweating, starving made his life no longer and no shorter.
Her hands should not imprison him, nor measure his
sustenance. He would love wildly and jealously, but in his
own heart. What nights he had spent wringing himself in
pain and grief, staring at the dark and shuddering with storm!
There was a goat's head with curling horns in the chasing of
his lamp. Wagging its head and staring from its lustful eyes,
it seemed to say:

'How the cloud of light would roll along her sides! She
would open to you like a gate.'

This was madness, hot and red and hellish. He looked out at her from every window: he shut every door upon her.

Blowing out the candle, he lay huddled on the bed, pinned and dying for the daybreak which would free his limbs and give his eyes a sight of reality. The last footfalls veered into silence: the last quarrelsome voices tacked home: the last blow fell and was forgotten. The wind rubbed the walls of the world. He was exhausted. He slept for a few hours and woke with a livid face and the acute throbbing above his eye, which was becoming more and more frequent. He was so sad—a sandbag was swinging under his heart, his head was dragged down. He could see the furniture in the room struggling through the ashy dawn. It grew around the candle like a stalk. The books in the rest on the mantelpiece were like a row of teeth all falling sideways. He was still dressed, his feet in woollen socks were uncovered and his arm, which in sleep he must have flung above his head, was dead to the shoulder. He lifted it with his other hand; it lay along his side like the arm of a corpse. His eyes ached and felt hot.

'I'm ill,' he said drearily.

Light was coming back, but there was nothing in the world to be revealed.

He lit the candle and lay passing his finger through the flame. Then he was thirsty. Painfully holding his forehead, he crept downstairs for a drink of water, and sat in the kitchen feeling too faint to move. He heard his stepmother roll away the chair which she always placed in front of her door at night, having lost the key. It was the only difference that the death of the policeman had made in her way of living.

The first thing he did when he had reached his room again was to lock his own door. Then he lay down groaning. A lorry passed, shaking his jug and basin. Soon the candle was stifled in daylight, but he forgot to put it out. The Mill syren shrieked at the end of the street.

The pain in his forehead was so intense that he dared not move, he was so desperately afraid of being sick. Obstinate, ghastly and helpless, his shirt open and his coat flung over his feet, he lay with clenched hands. Work had begun at the Mill.

At half-past seven Mrs. Rolfe came and rattled at his door:

'Bellamy, Bellamy, what's up with you?'

'I feel ill.'

'Aren't you going to work?'

'No.'

'I'll get a cup of tea.'

'I don't want tea. If you've got a lemon …'

'No, I haven't, but I'll get you a nice cup of tea. That'll pick you up.'

'No, it won't. It'll only make me sick,' said he.

'Is it your head?'

'Yes.'

'Then a cup of tea's the very thing. I'll bring it up this moment.'

But when she did, slopping it in the saucer, he would neither open his door nor answer her.

'Ungrateful little smut,' she muttered loudly with her lips to the keyhole, and left the cup outside the door, where later on she made the mistake of walking into it.

The brewery hooter went.

' If only I could go to sleep!' Bellamy thought, covering his eyes.

He was not sick. Little by little the pain went, leaving him tired, weak and indifferent. He washed himself, put on his overalls and combed his heavy hair. His eyes looked foggy and over him loomed the queer lost expression of mystic suffering. In the afternoon he went to work. The manager stared at him curiously.

'See here, you'd better go to the doctor or you'll be for kingdom come. Don't Mrs. Rolfe look after you?'

He saw Menna. She entered the yard and stood at the office door asking the clerk if he had seen her cat.

'No, I haven't,' he said, pursing his thick white lips: 'but there are all sorts o' pussies in here. There's plenty o' Tom cats, you see. Plenty o' young fellows, too,' he added genially.

Menna nodded jerkily to Bellamy and he turned away his head. She had seen him with Eileen Lewis.

*

Among others the Viking had stuck up a few small yellow bills announcing a boxing contest at the Harmony Club for the following night.

On that evening, when she had finished her shopping in the market, Menna wandered along the street with her basket on her arm until she was standing among a jostling group under the lamp outside the Harmony Club. There were men and women bantering and laughing:

'Hey, you got a bottle of dark down there?'

'No, it's a bottle of light.'

'Well, pass it along.'

'Does your husband drink beer?' a woman in a fur cap screamed.

'No, 'e eats it and thrives on it!'

Above their wagging heads with open mouths and rough

harsh-lit features sprang the tall building, blackish grey with yellow lighted windows. The empty street curved up to it smudged with shadows and greasy rain which fell in heavy single drops like black oil dripping from a vat. Menna heard it falling drop by drop on the taut umbrellas. As she stood there among the people, Bellamy Williams joined them with Eileen Lewis, stout and painted, her black hair crimped, breathing violet cachous into his ear. Once she had hit him, but Bellamy soon forgot her tempers because he was indifferent to her.

They showed two paper slips to the young man standing near the entrance and went in. Menna stepped forward.

'Only standing room left.'

'Can't get in here,' said the young man—'why, Menna, it's you. Only wish I could take you in meself. Here, Jeff,' he called inside, 'take this young lady round the back and see she gets a seat.'

Menna followed Jeff along a cobbled alley and up an iron staircase which clung to the brick wall. Bellamy had been smiling ... the rain shone on his forehead... .

Two wide doorways led into the hall. Menna's guide edged in until she found herself within a couple of yards of the ropes. She was upheld by men's chests and shoulders, and all around her were red, creased necks with sparse hairs growing above the collars. The ring was at one end of the long room, very white under the electric light. All the dim yet glowing faces were turned towards it, and a haze hung over everything, making it impossible to take in any detail of the watchers. The crowd seemed to have scooped a shallow dome in the darkness which sheltered them like roof and walls: they were knotted warmly together in smoke, sweat, breath and sawdust.

Surroundings they had none any more than sheep in a fold at night, where the shepherd's lantern wound in vapour dreams a circle on the ground and jigs among the rafters.

'I'm the only girl here. Oh, Bell, I do feel a fool!' Eileen whispered.

'Why? Shut up …' he muttered.

They both watched the fighting in complete ignorance of the names of the competitors, the prizes or any but the most obvious rules. All they saw and knew and understood was two under-sized squat men in black trunks—one had red stripes down the sides—hitting each other with great swollen gloves which left scarlet patches on their skin. The soft determined thump of the blows filled the hall, the men's breathing roared in their chests like burning gas. They sweated, their dainty dancing feet grew heavier—they were like two toads hopping round a stone. Jeering began:

'Put a ferrit in the ring!'

'A rabbit with a broken back 'ud jump cleaner.'

'God, it's the Salvation Army bazaar.'

'Go on—keep yer gloves up. God, look at 'is guard. 'E's all open—you could 'old a fair on 'im!'

Now the seconds were flapping towels before their sweating faces. Their heads were close-cropped with crescents of bare red skin behind the ears like the sweep of a scythe. Red Stripes' face was wiped: he nodded dully and let his head fall on his chest. His arms hung stiff from the shoulders.

Someone began to sing.

'Last round,' remarked the hoarse, knowing fellow who had been standing behind Menna and shouting over her shoulder: 'Oh, if 'e'll only keep is 'ands up 'e can 'it.'

But Red Stripes could not keep them up. His white chest

took all the blows. He sagged. The fight was over and they threw a thin towel over his shoulders.

With red-blotched bodies, shining muscles and sweat-drenched hair hanging over their foreheads, they climbed through the ropes and forced their way towards Bellamy and Eileen. As they shoved past him to get out, Bellamy's cold hand touched the hot wet skin; he twitched his arm and blinked. If *he* had been Red Stripes how he would have fought—with feet and teeth and ramming head!

These weren't *men*. These were 'sports' who didn't know what it was to feel savage rage in your limbs and strangulation in your heart. Bellamy felt himself go rolling over and over, clenching that wet streaky body, hugging the breath out of it, cracking its ribs against the reef of his own bones. To break a man against yourself—that must be joy, to fly, to fell a tree, to beat a woman whom you passionately desired, to go to war … perhaps to go to war … that was a future. Eileen was watching him unconsciously. What was he thinking? Did he ever think of asking her to marry him? She stroked her breast. The inside of her mouth was hot with the scent of violets.

Neither of them had seen Menna. She had drawn back against the wall, holding her basket high up under her chin. The men near her made jokes, eyed her, offered her a cigarette. She smoked and with every blow she saw landed her heart leapt fiercely as though she herself were hitting something which kept falling up against her. Eileen's cheek was near Bellamy's shoulder, the breath from her open lips drifted across him. Menna tore off her scarf and began to fan herself. For her all the spectacle was Bellamy: she *must* go to him and join her mouth to his. Her eyes were so terrible that many people noticed her.

Two sketchy youths went into the ring and flew at each other vigorously. Their panting breath burst from them, the light undulated on their backs. They whacked each other heartily, reeling against the ropes, their vests grey with sweat. Their flat shoes thumped the boards and the green paper fringe which was hanging over the window rustled and shivered like brittle leaves.

Bellamy rubbed the back of his neck.

'I call it rotten. If a fellow hit me I'd want to kill him and I'd try.'

'My word, that'd be worth watching!' giggled Eileen.

They stayed until the end. Bellamy was impatient and restless, but gradually the strong physical atmosphere, the noise of blows and feet, the hoarse murmurs from the audience, the pounding hearts of the fighters excited Eileen Lewis. She forgot to look at Bellamy or ask herself if he had thought of marriage. She crushed the bag of cachous between her fingers; her dark eyes were so widely opened that one could see the white staring all round the pupil. Menna, too, was affected by the criss-cross of the figures, and the spring of the boards under their insteps. They seemed to be struggling in her brain: a confusion of feelings oppressed her and she felt wild tears rising in her eyes. She was on the brink of a frenzy: the blows thudded like tribal drums in the caves of her ears. Her spirit was roused, crouched lower and lower, bent upon itself before it sprang. The present was a gulf to be leapt—her life eddied around her. She shut her jaws, her teeth felt as though they'd meet through iron.

A man was knocked out and lay athwart the ropes so near to her that she could see inside his open mouth. Blood dabbled his lip. *That* was what everybody was waiting for: they cheered, the shelves of faces rocked right and left. Bellamy quivered with rage. Had *he* been that man he thought that as soon as he had drawn his first lungful of air he'd have leapt up and bitten the nearest human he could reach—that chap in front of him, for instance, whose green waistcoat seemed on the point of bursting. Oh, how he hated everybody! he hated them with a mountain of contempt. Menna was looking at him … she had only one desire and that was to be with him. 'If he doesn't come to me, I shall go to him.'

It was over: music was turned on suddenly—the order of the place was turned upside down as if the hall had been given a violent shake. To the insinuating shuffle of a rumba the audience began to labour towards the doors. They moved slowly down the iron stairs like thick liquid oozing from a bottle, grasping the hand-rail with wet fingers, clustering at the bottom in a patch of light thrown upwards from a basement window, tossing their faces towards the chimneys and the pitch blackness of the sky.

Bellamy and Eileen walked down to Mill End arm-in-arm. The fried fish bar was full of people, reeking of hot oil and vinegar and spilling its trade upon the street. A side door was open: Eileen dragged Bellamy inside and leaning her two arms against the wall, flung back her head for the kiss she burned to feel.

'If we weren't strangers I'd hate you,' he said. 'I hate myself. I wish that I could fight myself. I can't get at it, I can't, I can't,' he cried despairingly.

'Kiss me, Bell…'

'I can't, I can't,' he cried and burst away from her, and all along Mill Street went crying madly, with his fists clenched to his brows as one grinding a stone into the earth.

Mrs. Rolfe was sewing in the kitchen, her feet planted heavily half a yard apart on the striped mat. His supper was on the table covered with a newspaper. But he flung off to bed. Bundling her work under a cushion, she gave a tug to her sleeves, rolled back the mat and raked out the fire. The goat on the lamp seemed to be watching her and saying: 'I never had much to do with you and now nothing.'

Bellamy did not sleep. Lying on his elbow, his head bowed near the lighted candle, he wrote a letter to Menna.

'I can't reach you, my love. I can't get near you. There's nothing I can give you if you won't first take me. Dear, my dear, nothing and nobody means anything to me but you and the places where I've been with you I'll never forget. Is it impossible for you to love me? If it is I can't exist here in such despair. I must go away. I must leave the Mill.

'I shall enlist. I was at the Harmony Club to-night, watching the fighting and it made me think of the army.

'Oh, what can I do, and where can I go when you are in me always, but die? I have no rest. My dearest, my darling, I am going. Let me see you once.'

At the other end of the street, Menna, too, was awake. Since she had seen Bellamy she had been in agony, not knowing whether to go to him or whether he was Eileen's now. That he would ever love Eileen as he had loved herself she was certain would never be; but perhaps it was too late to tell him that she knew, that for days past she had never thought of her mother save to hope that she would die as she herself hoped to live.

It had stopped raining: indeed, it never rained continuously now, as if the elements themselves were tired of their sameness. There would be a scurrying downpour, then a dark interval while the clouds flew overhead, vanished behind the hills, and rushed on them again from the western ramparts where the winter sun was stifling in brassy mists. A raw wind clung to the streets and spiralled in the gutters.

The curtain was shaking. The window panes were black like ice against the shutter outside, each clear in the centre and foggy in the corners: the warm air condensed on the glass, the lamp standing on the counter shone with a deadened light upon the coats and dresses hanging all around the shop. It seemed as though the light were turned back into the globe and muffled with heavy folds. It was days since customers had been in; the shutters were always closed, the counter was bare except for an empty oilcan.

The house was silent and hopeless. Nothing struggled between its walls, behind its shutters. The end was approaching like night. Even the dust lay undisturbed: the fires were kindled over ashes, the light and dark passed over the windows like shadows, sounds were raised up in silence like sand in the desert and settled again in unchanged loneliness and solitude. A bunch of keys lay on the kitchen table unnoticed, untouched, put there by Mrs. Trouncer days before, as if she had done with locks and secrecy. One locks only air from air.

She lay in bed on her back, her hands under her head, her eyes closed. Endless chambers of darkness opened under the lids, tunnels of distance bored into her brain. She was walking into space through her sight, and then she would throw out her hands to fend away the rushing figures which fled along the walls like a tide pushing against the inevitable advance of her consciousness towards the nothing at the end. Her thirst was like terror; it came upon her with shudders, horrors and sweating; and then feeling the bed slant under her like a raft tossed on a wave, she dragged herself up with daggers in her temples and drank the whisky which her daughter had bought for her. The implacable dispositions and capabilities which she had kindled in Menna's soul condemned her to die on what had killed her. The girl was a murderess in love. With no counsel, no consolation, no company, she fought for her right to her own remorse. In the last two weeks she had thrown off the stone upon her head and assumed the proportions of her predestined deed.

Benjamin Wandby had rightly judged that she had no pity, but only a lover's compassion. She waited for the release which she had hastened. *She* burned, too, *she* battled underneath the silence, she longed for her lover in the month which she had demanded and made like a wheel to turn her fate and his. And when she saw him with Eileen Lewis she suffered defeat and the anguish of victory answering no strong purpose. She felt no guilt. *She* would die, if later, not easier. *Her* life stood to be struck as she had stricken. Her own nature told her the secrets of all.

And dust lay on this! And silence held to its foundations in this quaking house and did not totter. Nature recognizes her extreme necessities and shelters their fulfilments under her impregnable decrees. It's the wanton idiotic and motiveless action which stands up like a mountain in daylight with the perpetrator babbling and pointing his finger at the singularity.

Bellamy pushed his letter under the door on his way to work at seven in the morning. Menna was still in the shop, her head leaning on the counter. She raised herself, sighed and pushed back her hair. She was thin and ghastly: every hour of the night had left its wake upon her face. She had quenched the lamp, and it was not yet light, though the street was busy and the hooters were sounding. By the light of a match she read her letter, looked over it, ravenous, wild and keen without a sign of sleep. She gave a cry, groped for the bolt and was outside. She ran to the Mill. Bellamy was in the office talking to the clerk. She could see him through the glass door standing near the desk in his overalls, his hand on the back of the clerk's chair, his profile cut in the green wall. She knocked.

'Come in.'

'No, come out!' she cried through the glass.

'Bellamy, do you love me?' she asked when he was with her.

'Why do you ask me? I would have said it if you had given me time.'

'You love me and not Eileen Lewis?'

'I love you and nobody else on earth.' He seized her hand and pressed it to his eyes as if he were sinking in vertigo. 'Where can I meet you, Menna? Listen, will you come round to me? The old woman's out, and won't be back till late.'

She nodded. They stared at each other and simultaneously tore apart and ran in opposite directions. She seemed to rush into a cloud: he felt the cold air in his veins like blood, and seized a trolley in the empty tallet and trundled it over the hollow mealy floor round and round until its rumble trod out the rhythms of the engines in his ears, and it seemed that all the houses must fall flat with joy, and all men be deafened by their brimming hearts!

By evening he was languid with longing. He drew the curtains close over the windows. His certain waiting was ecstasy.

He left the door open and stood in the passage looking down the street where women and children were going errands with coats flung over their heads, fetching fish for supper and cider in cans. No men were about: they had their feet up, their boots off and their faces stuck in the *Chepsford Gazette*. It was while he had his eyes turned in the other direction that Menna came; while he was thinking that the shape of the gas-works was like a furnace door from the side seams of which burst the sparkle of stars ruptured in space and trailing light on the smoky clouds.

It was seven o'clock.

'How late you are!' he said sadly; 'you'll be gone so soon.'

She shook her head. Her mouth was trembling, her eyes wandered in their wan sockets. She stared and stared at him, stared in bewilderment as if she were bewitched.

She sat down on a low chair. Bellamy kneeled on the floor drawing her cold fingers through his lips. He kept asking her if she loved him:

'You'll have to tell me many, many times before I can believe it.'

'Why don't you put your head on my knees?' she barely murmured.

'I didn't know you'd let me.'

There was a shocking second of suspense. Then helplessly, finally, he let his head fall on her lap. She stooped to him and laid him between her breasts, and loosed her love to go out to him. She pressed him into her, and her mouth broke like a wave.

All night she was with him. She showed him the key of the house, like a pledge, and they put it under the pillow. Bellamy's bedroom was cold as death, with a sweat of damp on the low ceiling, the rug askew, the slops unemptied, the bed wrinkled and the bolster on the floor.

'Mrs. Rolfe left early. She's tired of me and wants me to get out.'

They lay on the bed making warmth for each other, impervious to everything outside. They lolled like gods on a peak of peace. Arms widespread on the tumbled clothes, she kissed him:

'Oh, my darling, what should I do if I never saw you again? I'm afraid. Come to me. I'm mad now. Kiss me. Kiss my heart.'

From head to heel he clothed her naked body with caresses. Her hair hid her eyelids: her nakedness was tangled in the candle-light and the shadows.

He opened his eyes and closed them with a single look of love. He was asleep.

She watched the dawn on his face. It seemed to rise from him, to break through the skin, like the loosened spirit lifting in the air. It might have been burning from some jet within the head, which seemed sleep in concrete, wrought and sealed in a statue. The hair fell back from the blank forehead and the neck lay like a fallen pillar.

Grey lines were running up the wall. This was day in a cage reaching out a slow limb. But suddenly he woke and, shooting out his hand at the window, cried out in terror:

'I've been asleep and wasted you! oh God Almighty it is morning and you'll be gone, and I have been asleep!'

There was in his bold upright body some queer struggle of benighted strange incorporeal passion.

'I love you, I love you, I love you! Whatever happens I will love you. I *wish* you grew on me. I wish there were no flesh between us. There must be peace. Oh, Menna, I can never, never show you … I can only feel it *here*!'

'I know, I know. Light the candle and let me see your face again before I go.'

In the light they looked at each other. Only their eyes moved. She leaned upon her arms, gazing down at him. Her shadow brooded on the wall.

'You can never escape me,' he said.

No, only the past was empty of him. Among her frightful memories there were none of him, thank heaven. To look at him was to see a new beginning built upon her passion and her inflexible resolution.

She pulled down the blind and dressed in a hurry, folding her coat close over her carelessly fastened clothes. She rinsed her face in cold water. The little room was full of movement, and the draughts made by her quick, silent steps. The bed vibrated when she set the jug on the floor. She threw the towel over her shoulders and passed his comb through her hair. He sat up on his elbow watching her. And suddenly he yawned, and laughed, yawned again and got out of bed. He put out his arm and grasped her waist. 'Kiss me. I feel you've torn yourself away from something. Do you really love me?'

'I'm sure of it,' she answered breathlessly. 'I was a fool.'

They.kissed goodbye.

'When you go to work I'll be in the shop. Stop and speak to me,' she said.

She stole downstairs, unbolted the door and stepped out into the street. The cold rose up to her knees. She looked up at the blind shut window and hurried away…

As she walked down the street with her head bent to keep the cold wind off her neck, she had a sense of attempting to fit ordinary life on to the happiness of a dream. It was as if she were trying to join the two, and feeling curiously nonexistent in the body, that she stood in front of her own door seeing nothing but Bellamy's cold room with the warm, disordered bed before her eyes. She too yawned and smiled.

She stretched her arms in the empty street. Her expanded breast felt like a great open plain.

The door was not locked. Why?

She felt discovered. She was astounded. Who could have been out or in? Her mother … her uncle from Salus?

She went in. Of all the people she would least have expected to see there stood the one, Francis Dollbright, in an overcoat, holding a candle up to light her way into the kitchen. Benjamin Wandby was there, too. They stared at her, fraught with calamity, while she clutched her coat around the memory of her nakedness and thought that one at least would call her night shameful.

'I don't know what you're doing here,' she said uncertainly.

'Don't be frightened; nobody's broken in,' Benjamin assured her, while his eyes passed gravely over her disturbed face; 'but we have bad news for you. Your mother has had a very serious accident. She has been taken to the hospital.'

'Is she dying?'

'I'm afraid so,' they said together, and Dollbright continued:

'We can't say, of course. The doctor thought it was very serious. She was unconscious.'

He added:

'At least, I think she was. She spoke to me, but she was delirious, I should say. She didn't seem to see me.'

'What did she say?'

He hesitated.

' "I'm dying, I'm dying and I want somebody to love me," ' he said in a low voice, turning away from her.

'But I did!' she screamed.

The two men were standing close together when suddenly she threw up her arms and smashed through them with a blind impetus as though she were hurling herself off a height, her teeth bare, her face distorted and broken up by an awful muscular grimace. She rushed right into the wall, her hands above her head and they heard her nails scratch against the whitewash.

'I have killed her! Oh God, let her die, let her be dead now and I'll believe in right.'

'Menna, turn round and look at us. Look at me. I don't blame you,' said Benjamin sternly: 'if you *have* killed her, what was she doing to you? What has she been doing to you ever since you were born? You have lived with her all your life; who but she can have made you what *you* are? I tell you this isn't pity but justice. Turn round and face us, for you have every right to meet anyone's eyes.'

'Turn round, there's no blame here. It's your birthmark,' said Dollbright: 'we have ours.'

Benjamin gaped at him, astonished beyond all measure at such words and tone from *him* of all men. He caught hold of his beard and his face, with open mouth turned from side to side as if his slowly rolling eyes were searching for the reason in the empty air.

He and Dollbright had been sitting for three hours without speaking. He had supposed that Dollbright was waiting with condemnation ready, and he was determined to be with her and defend her against the 'Archangel.'

He admitted that he had never known Dollbright go out of

his way to judge people—he was not a scavenger of sin—but those who fell or stumbled near him he noticed and condemned without acrimony or mercy. He was just, according to his peculiar beliefs. A just man. But that itself implied a bias in his character, since the duty of justice is to punish vices but not to discover virtues.

'Come, sit down, Menna,' he said, taking her by the hand and leading her to the settle.

'Don't cry,' Benjamin begged as she covered her eyes, and unable to refrain from touching her, he stooped and caressed her head. But she flung him off angrily.

'Cry!' she uttered furiously, 'I'm not crying. I never have. That's one of the privileges of people who have friends to comfort them. You can go out in the street and pity anyone you meet, but don't spend it on *me*. I pity myself and I shan't leave off, because *now* it's happened you come and tell me what I've known for fifteen years. You seem to think you've made a discovery: you seem to think I'm sorry: I tell you I hope she's dead.'

The two men drew back from her while she glared at them across the hearth.

'She's right; it's our fault. What use are we now?' said Benjamin slowly and heavily.

'How often have you left your mother since you've lived here?' he asked.

'This once,' she sullenly replied.

'It was the will of God,' Dollbright thought. He was walking up and down the kitchen. 'And yet you found time to help us when my wife was in hospital.'

To this she returned no answer. Apparently she could not forgive Benjamin for supposing she was in tears.

'Cry!' she repeated contemptuously, 'you don't cry to a wall. I've been here through whole black winters, and if I wanted to see a human face I looked in the mirror for it. Mother's wasn't human. You thought it bad enough if you saw her outside; but what would you have thought if you had seen *into* her—if you'd heard her say the things she saw? If she's dead they're dead with her and I'm glad … I'm glad! But I must be dead too before I can forget them!'

There was an inward stare in her fixed eyes which seemed not to see but to feel submerged terrors. She no longer noticed them. She talked with her steady gaze on one patch in the middle of the floor.

'Don't stop her—it will ease her mind,' Benjamin whispered. But:

'Muffle thy hammer, oh Almighty God!' Dollbright prayed.

'Perhaps they are not dead; perhaps they are real. So how can her dying kill them? She only saw them, and I see these flag-stones; but if I'm dead they are still there. Hell, hell! I went to Sunday School, and they said: "God made the world in six days and made rest in one." That's why there is so little rest, such late peace…I love Bellamy; but if I remembered him as far back as this, and part of it, I'd hate him too… .'

She stopped, and, parched for relief, they saw at last that she was crying.

'Shall we go now?' Dollbright sought advice from Benjamin.

'No, no, not yet. She had better be told how it happened. She will be asked. Leave her alone for a little.'

After a minute or two he inquired in a very matter-of-fact, everyday voice whether she would make them some tea. They were very thirsty and cold.

She got up at once, dried her eyes and went to fill the kettle. When she came back she said:

'Thank you for being here. I don't understand what happened. When I left mother she was lying in bed. Did she fall down stairs?'

'No,' Dollbright answered: 'she must have got down safely. But the cellar trap was open—'

He stopped with a garbled gesture and turned away his face. Presently he resumed.

'I was late going to bed last night, or rather this morning. I suppose it was about two o'clock, when I happened to look out of our kitchen window, and I thought I saw a light at the end of the alley. I didn't hurry to go and see what it was, because I felt sure it must be you. But five or ten minutes after it was still there, so I went outside, and it was a lantern lying on the ground, but still burning. Then I ran; your mother was on the cellar steps, about halfway down, with her dress caught on a nail….'

'What… what had she done to herself? How was she hurt?'

'The back of her head and … her arm is broken. She must have fallen on it… .'

'Don't stop—go on. I did it,' Menna groaned, a grinding in her voice.

She walked to the window and pulled back the curtain, then put out the candle. They were all standing in the tawny light of a stormy morning with snow piling up in the yellow sky.

'I did it; but I didn't want her to be hurt like that. Go on … go on.'

'What have I told you? I forget,' said Dollbright unsteadily. He was walking up and down again. The untouched tea grew cold on the table. Benjamin was holding his head in his hands. They all heard a knocking on the street door.

'It's Bellamy. I spent the night with him, and he's on his way to work,' she said.

Dollbright paused, made an awkward sound and resumed his pacing, his eyes fixed on the stove pipe disappearing through a sooty hole in the wall.

'Are you going to let him in?'

'No!'

'I should. I think you'd better,' said Benjamin.

'No,' she repeated violently.

'Why not? He'll have to be told. There'll be an inquest, Menna, certain to be.'

'I will not let him in, nor open the door, nor speak to him,' she said doggedly; 'if there's an inquest *they* may let him in to it, I can't help that, I'm not dumb or a liar, but I'll use all my strength to bolt him out of this until they drag him in. So *knock* until you think I'm asleep and don't want to wake me,' she concluded, shutting her fist on her breast while the knocking went on. Then it stopped. Bellamy had gone on to work.

'But why—why! In God's name, Menna, what's come into your mind?' cried Benjamin searchingly.

'It's fantastic devotion,' Dollbright said at utter loss.

'Devotion to myself, then,' she retorted: 'you fools, can't you understand? Haven't you anything to remember that you can't forget? … or not so much forget as live out of yourself? And would you mix your happiness with that? Unless you were a suicide, would you mix poison in your own food? I'm going to marry Bellamy—I'm going to begin from him.'

'You can't do it, Menna,' said Benjamin, trembling, 'who knows it better than I do?

'I can. I have,' she answered unshaken, 'it's my purpose

and I *will* carry it out. Listen! For two years Bellamy and I have loved each other, and all that time I never opened my mind to him but once, and that three weeks ago. I never talked of mother to him, I never let him in with her, so when I thought of him I didn't see her face behind him! It's too late to tell me when I've done it, that it can't be done. That's the door he'll never break—it's in the middle of me and I've nailed it up both sides!'

For her sake, Benjamin choked the bloody denial on his lips: 'Well, go on. May you be right. You seem strong,' he said.

And he too turned away from her in bitter thought. In order not to keep too close a watch upon her, they stood their distance over by the window.

The virulence and passion sank down in her. She sat in an attitude of log-like indifference, heavy and inert, pressing her hands into her knees, all her looks dull and sullen, her hair hanging over her white cheeks like sad dangling weeds.

A few small snowflakes floated past the window. They were all silent.

But sudden and sharp the memory of the night before throbbed in her and, with secret joy, she defied Benjamin's croaking.

Presently she lifted her head and asked them to finish telling her of her mother's accident.

'I have told you almost everything,' said Dollbright: 'when I found her lying on the steps I ran for Mr. Wandby. We wrapped her in rugs as well as we could because we couldn't lift her up the steps; besides, I was afraid of moving her. And then he looked for you all over the house, while I stayed with her.'

'We told the doctor you were away,' said Benjamin: 'we had to break open the door to let him in. He sent for the ambulance.'

'Good! Now I shall know what to say,' she exclaimed resolutely.

'Oh, I find myself strange!' Dollbright burst out, and once more he began to move erratically around the room, as if indeed the spring in him were broken or damaged by repeated strains.

'You want to tell the truth, I suppose,' said Menna.

'No, no, I don't. I wouldn't do it—that's what's strange,' Dollbright muttered.

The two men left the Trouncers house at eight o'clock after some further discussions and arrangements.

'You're surely not going to work?' Benjamin asked, peering into Dollbright's exhausted face with his short-sighted, bloodshot eyes.

'Yes, I'm better at my desk than anywhere else,' he answered sadly.

'I can't help feeling awfully guilty,' Benjamin stammered.

'Yes, I know.'

Morning and afternoon went by. The sky was the colour of trampled snow and hung over the town like a cloth weighted with stones. The hills were swaddled, the air deadened. The yellow sulphurous atmosphere seemed to bring with it a thick impediment to sound through which footsteps and dim voices struggled fitful and imperfect as though behind a door.

The lamps were alight by two o'clock and burned like a row of candles in a crypt. A patch of brick loomed up behind each one and dissolved imperceptibly into the mist. Here and there the vertical line of a building defined left and right and stood up as vertebras in the boneless air.

From his desk Dollbright watched the hoarding opposite gradually blur and disappear; above an area grating the vapour rose like steam; the passers-by wove large vague outlines and marched in the dimness with the potency of striding gods.

While man's soul entertains the lineal universe his eye creeps beetle-wise over the earth; and Dollbright, though dreadfully aware of an upheaving in the planks of that creed which he had trod so heavily, though aware that for some time they had moved stormily and breached apart and threatened to fail him altogether, yet kept himself together by nailing his eyesight to hard surface details and reckoning figures.

But it was too mechanical: his work was as good as ever, his health improved and his existence settled; but the processes of realization were not checked by the effort. He had begun to think, and by God, he had to go on. And circumstances instead of plastering up the cracks, undermined the disintegration. He could find no conclusion to rest upon, nor, what was worse, could he define his wordless doubts.

A week or two ago, Florence, remarking that he was silent and in heavy spirits, and no longer went to church nor took to chapel, and suffering from a superstitious fear of what his impiety might bring on them in the way of worldly misfortune, had secretly sent her minister to him in the hope that he might inspire her husband with the same 'steadfast faith' which had supported her through her operation.

As usual, Mr. Tielard concealed his effrontery beneath a manner of superficial embarrassment. Dollbright remembered his own indignation and involuntary sophistry with a grim laugh. One could *not* reveal oneself to such absurd people. The interview came tripping back to him.

'Good afternoon, Mr. Dollbright,' the minister ejaculated.

'You mustn't resent my little call or take it as anything but a simple friendly visit. We ministers have privileges which are most kindly tolerated by our friends, as we know, and we must avail ourselves of them.' He grimaced.

He seemed to see Mr. Tielard so plainly!

'Now I can put the purpose of my visit in a very few words, quite simply, so that you will understand that I really want to help. Eh, your wife tells me that you don't go to church or chapel?'

'That is so.'

'Of course, if you went to church I shouldn't dream of interfering—I respect all faiths, Mr. Dollbright—but since you are at a loose end, may I try to make myself clear by a little parable?'

'By all means,' he grimly answered.

'Ah! Well, if I see a flock of sheep in the fold I am not justified in taking one to my own fold. That would be unnecessary.'

'That would be stealing.'

'Eh? Oh, yes… . But if I see one loose in the fields without a shepherd, I am doing wisely to enclose it with my own.'

'I doubt it,' said Dollbright woodenly, 'it might lead to legal entanglements.'

The minister was plainly disconcerted by this reception of his favourite allegory.

'Putting legal quibbles aside and considering it spiritually— I *am*,' he persisted.

'Well, granted, though it seems rather risky. What then?'

'Well, don't you understand? Let me be more plain: it is quite clear that God does not wish man to stand alone.'

'No, he made him a wife.'

'Yes,' said the minister eagerly, 'to lead him.'

'She led him into evil. You have either forgotten man's fall, Mr. Tielard, or wilfully over-looked certain truths in it. Didn't God first conceive man as standing alone?'

'Yes, but—'

'He did!'

Suddenly losing command of himself, he shouted: 'Man, have you seen God? Did he send you to me? Did he tell you that I was a sinner? Did He hide from *me* and report my faults to *you*! Do you confess to such a grovelling idea of God and such a high one of yourself? Next time you open your mouth remember Lucifer fell!'

The recollection turned on him with a bitter sting as he remembered how he had reproved Ifor Morriss. He thought with astonishment: 'I couldn't do that now.'

And his own answers to the minister came back to him with a new significance as though he had been speaking more truly and profoundly than he guessed.

Old Williams banged on the partition: 'Here, Dollbright, aren't you going home? 'Ave you forgot it's early closing?'

'Presently. I'll stay a little while. Give me the keys and I'll lock up.'

'My baby's going to be married. Blame me he is! Came in this morning and told me. Didn't you see 'im?'

'No, I've been so busy.'

The old man put on his cap and went out.

'Snowing,' he shouted. His face approached the smeary panes from the outside and he grinned and nodded crazily. Dollbright realized he was itching with delight at the thought of his son's wedding. He shuddered.

Yes, it was snowing. The flakes drifted without weight or

impetus towards the earth. Already they had gathered in the leads. He could only see through two small patches in the centre of each pane, and a white rayless light fell on his desk. He turned off the electric light. There was no traffic, no sound at all. It seemed as if everything were wrapped in felt.

He remembered again.

He saw himself stooping over the monstrous figure lolling brokenly on the black mouldy steps, its garment slowly, slowly tearing from a nail. He smelled the horrible odour of drink and dirt and decay mixed with slimy wood and the rawness of stored potatoes. The hideous incident paused in his mind's eye, invoking horror, sickness … and deep unaccustomed pity. What staggering enforced journey had plunged into that dark earthy hole with the fallen lantern shining on the brink? What whole abandonment by every human soul had she discovered in the night? She spoke of love?

Unlike Benjamin, he was less affected by the tragedy of Menna's development than by her mother's ghastly end. She had crashed across his unchosen track like a lightning-stricken tree whose shadow was consumed by fire and death. This was her act in his destiny. This was the power over him which he had felt with a super-natural shrinking from the inevitable demonism of her eye, the demoniacal authority of her wild, half-hinted speech, which was subterraneously linked to the breaking forth of his own fierce ungoverned spirit.

That spirit had moved him all his life. Pounded down, subdued and overloaded, leashed and lashed by his inexorable unnatural faith, he had struggled to make of that restless genitor a sacrifice to eternity. And it had burst upwards under his feet. And he had quoted it before he knew that he had heard its gagged voice speak. He had cited it to a fool who thought himself miraculously familiar with heaven and the fixed appointments of the enigmatic influences good and evil.

He laid his face and laughed relentlessly as he recalled propounding the unconscious workings of his spirit to the minister who recognized men only as the patient sheep in the pastures of the Father's palm—to be shorn, to be slain, to be plucked from the wolf, to furnish the insatiable pride of the altar…

For a long time he had not thought at all. Every day he had come and gone to his work, he had sat with his wife, he had suffered the terrible nothing in his breast and his brain. Last night, with blood on his hand and holding the matted head up on his arm, he had felt a great opening in his mind as though air were rushing into a vacuum. He could not think then: he was almost strangled, speechless in thought and undelivered.

Now words were working in him, excitement seized him. He felt his existence enclosed in a tremendous destiny. The knots in his breast relaxed in a rushing thaw. He shouted wildly, he walked about the empty shop in the snowlight like a man clean mad, possessed by freedom.

'I can lament or defy. And I'm defiant. From your millions you have lost me, and all your aeons will never bring me back. Order could not compel me; pain shall not subdue me, and tears are not repentance. The more powerful you, the weaker I; but the more you gather the less you never lose! Oh God, I have taken separate existence from you, and you cannot pour my one soul back into your self!'

It grew dusky with a white, blind twilight, like the film of cataract. Benjamin Wandby came and knocked at the window. Dishevelled, passionate, Dollbright stood in the door.

'I thought I'd find you here,' said the other; 'I've come to tell you she's dead.'

'Dead, dead?' he echoed like a foreign word. He was free of death.

THE END

ABOUT HONNO

Honno Welsh Women's Press was set up in 1986 by a group of women who felt strongly that women in Wales needed wider opportunities to see their writing in print and to become involved in the publishing process. Our aim is to develop the writing talents of women in Wales, give them new and exciting opportunities to see their work published and often to give them their first 'break' as a writer. Honno is registered as a community co-operative. Any profit that Honno makes is invested in the publishing programme. Women from Wales and around the world have expressed their support for Honno. Each supporter has a vote at the Annual General Meeting. For more information and to buy our publications, please write to Honno at the address below, or visit our website: www.honno.co.uk

Honno, 14 Creative Units, Aberystwyth Arts Centre
Aberystwyth, Ceredigion SY23 3GL

Honno Friends

We are very grateful for the support of the Honno Friends: Jane Aaron, Annette Ecuyere, Audrey Jones, Gwyneth Tyson Roberts, Beryl Roberts, Jenny Sabine.

For more information on how you can become a Honno Friend, see: http://www.honno.co.uk/friends.php